A HEART WELL TRAVELED
VOLUME 3

A HEART WELL TRAVELED
VOLUME 3

EDITED BY SALLYANNE MONTI

SAPPHIRE BOOKS

SALINAS, CALIFORNIA

Preface

Journey through Africa, Australia, Bora Bora, Canada, Europe, the Middle East, South America and the United Kingdom, as lovers traverse the paths of change and challenge, to be with their one true love.

The characters will take you on a whirlwind ride, from secret love affairs to chance encounters as they face the inevitable reality of a broken heart or a happy ending.

This exhilarating anthology will leave you affected and inspired, as far away places come to life while the characters break down borders and boundaries, to be together forever.

Can they defy the odds?
Sallyanne Monti, Editor

Acknowledgment

A Heart Well Traveled Volume 3

This is Volume Three in Sapphire Books' long distance romance anthology series, A Heart Well Traveled.

This series is made possible by the contributions of the stellar group of authors, who bring unique style and imagination to the project. Heartfelt thanks, to all the authors who entrusted their stories to us.

Much gratitude extended to Ann McMan and Treehouse Studios for the cover art that so beautifully highlighted the theme in each of the volumes while tying the series together with parallel artistic design, and to LJ Reynolds for book design that compliments the engaging nature of the stories.

Sincere appreciation extended to Sapphire Books and Publisher Christine Svendsen, who enthusiastically encourages creative expression while fostering literary distinction.

It's been an honor to partner with all the talented professionals on this project.

Sincerely,
Sallyanne Monti, Editor

Table of Contents

Lady Kisses

By C. L. Cattano

Cherie stepped off the train into the chaos of the Milan Central terminal and waited patiently for the attendant to unload the luggage. She claimed the pieces that belonged to her and then pulled them along to get off the boarding platform and into the station proper. It was her first trip to Italy. She would be staying with Nolita, the woman she had forged an online relationship with over the past year. To say Cherie was anxious was an understatement. What if when they met, there was nothing between them or if the expectation in her head did not match reality? She stopped directly under the clock as they'd agreed and then searched the crowd for the face of the woman she loved.

After an hour Cherie was on the brink of feeling devastated. Waiting any longer would make it difficult to find a hotel. Being patient for another quarter hour, Cherie decided it was time to find a place with internet access where she could check her computer.

A few blocks from the train station Cherie found a café that advertised free Wi-Fi and pulled her luggage inside. After ordering a coffee and a delicious looking pastry, she found a table. She tried not to cry as she got online and sent an email to Nolita. It was possible that they missed each other or there was a miscommunication somehow. There was even the possibility that something tragic had happened. It was hard to believe that Nolita would purposely leave her in this situation. She decided to wait a bit longer before admitting defeat and accepting she was in a foreign country, stranded. The waitress brought her order to the table. Cherie took a fortifying sip of coffee. Her only solace was the pastry was heavenly.

It was dark outside. Cherie had tried many things from the café menu. However, she had not received a reply to the plea for help sent to Nolita. Cherie was getting desperate. To make matters worse, the only accommodation she found was a shared hostel room with twelve other people. Cherie hoped to find something better. She looked around noting that the café was about to close. Wiping tears from her cheeks, she packed up her computer. Cherie had no idea what to do now. She might have to sleep in the train station or contact the embassy to see if they had a place for unlucky travelers.

"Pardon, are you finished?" asked the waitress.

"Oh." Cherie sniffed. "Yes," she said. She pushed her dishes toward the woman.

"Is everything all right?"

"Yes," she said quickly. "No." She tried unsuccessfully to hold back tears.

"Can you tell me what's happened?" asked the waitress. She had a lovely Italian accent.

"The person I was supposed to meet hasn't shown up. I have nowhere to go. I've been trying to find a hotel but everywhere is full."

"Yes." The waitress nodded. "It is the fashion shows. They come and fill up everything."

"Great." Cherie sighed.

"My name is Valoria." She held her hand out.

She shook Valoria's hand and said, "Cherie."

"If you want, you can rent the spare room I have at my house."

"Really?" Cherie was shocked that Valoria would rent her room to a stranger. She was not sure if she should take the offer or not. What if the place was worse than the hostel or she was an Italian homicidal maniac?

"Si, I need the money, you need a place to stay." Valoria shrugged as if it was the most normal thing in the world. "It's good," she said.

⁂

Valoria had been watching the woman since she dragged her ridiculously large pieces of luggage into the café. She took up a significant amount of real estate for such a small woman and certainly didn't spend enough money to justify the area she had claimed and the free Wi-Fi she was using. It was a good thing she decided to speak with her. If she had not, the woman would be out on the streets of Milan tonight. Fortunately, Valoria had to deliver pastries and desserts that morning and had driven her car to work. Otherwise, it would have been a harrowing trek into the underground and a battle to get through the masses that filled the platforms and the rail cars with all of her luggage.

After they had lumbered into the house with the luggage, Valoria showed Cherie around. "You can use what you like," she said, as they entered the sparkling clean kitchen. "Only don't use the food in this refrigerator. That is for my business."

"What business do you have?"

"I'm a pastry chef. I get orders from a few places around town. I'm just working at the café until I can open my shop. I feel like it's taking forever."

"I know how that feels!" Cherie was pleased that they had something in common. "Back home I own three food trucks. We specialize in bringing gourmet food in street food style. I've been considering doing a dessert food truck but haven't found a chef that's the right fit. I never went to school for it though. I'm what you call a grandma-taught-chef." She chuckled at her joke. "But I do know the food business, so I guess that's why I've been successful. I'm hoping to open a brick and mortar store someday too. I just want a small place somewhere in my community." She blushed realizing she had been talking way too much.

"Food trucks sound fun. I feel like a food car sometimes." Valoria smiled, glad Cherie seemed in better spirits. "We have some good ones in Milan."

"I'll look for them. I like trying new foods."

"So, do you know why your friend never showed up? You can use my phone to call if you'd like. It would be great if you stayed because as I said, I could use the money, but I understand if you go with your friend."

Cherie sat at the kitchen table, her mood swinging back toward despair. "I probably should try to call her. I hope she's okay."

"Here." Valoria handed the phone trying not to raise her eyebrows at the fact Cherie was meeting another woman. She stopped herself from prying. "Call her. It's rude to make visitors wait."

Cherie pulled out her itinerary with the number she had written at the top. After a few rings, a message in Italian announced that the voice mailbox was full.

She was afraid that would happen. It happened when Nolita turned her phone off or let the battery die.

Cherie looked up at Valoria. "No answer just like the email I sent."

"Maybe there are problems because of the fashion events. I'm surprised your friend wanted you to come at this time. Every year the entire town is put out." She laughed trying to be reassuring. "But it's good for me because I have a lot of orders to fill." She looked in the smaller refrigerator that held her food. "I don't have a lot here. We can walk to the market, or we can eat out. Milan is full of lovely restaurants."

"I think it'd be fun to shop for food in Italy," said Cherie, glad to have someone who could read the labels. Cherie was grateful for at least three things today—the pastries, the room, and the company of a new friend.

❧ ❧ ❧ ❧

Cherie woke to the smell of something baking. She looked at the clock and was surprised Valoria was already up after their late night of talking about food over wine. Wiping the sleep from her eyes, Cherie trotted down the stairs still in her pajamas. She entered the kitchen just as Valoria pulled a baking tray from the oven.

"Good morning," she yawned.

"Bondi," said Valoria. "A typical Italian morning greeting for you to learn."

"Already teaching me the language? I didn't know I'd be thinking this early."

"I have an order to deliver, and I have to work a half day at the café. Would you like some caffé?"

"Yes, thank you." She watched Valoria scoop

coffee into the top of a silver coffee pot and set it on the stove to boil. "I get a homemade espresso? I'm glad I got up while you were still here."

"This is the best way to make caffé." She slid another tray into the oven then continued to box baked goods. When she finished boxing, Valoria poured the caffé and placed it and a plate of small cookies in front of Cherie. "I am known for these cookies. They are called *Bachi di Dama*. I don't make these at the café unless they order them special."

"Delicious!" Cherie could not help her outburst. The cookies were divine. Each was a perfect bite of crispness and hazelnut with a center of semi-sweet chocolate. She could see herself becoming addicted if not careful.

"I do some custom fillings too, but most people are happy with chocolate."

"I would try them all if I didn't know for a fact they would go straight to my hips." She looked at all the trays ready to go in the oven. "*Bachi di*...what was it?" She wanted to remember it for her dessert food truck.

"*Bachi di Dama*," Valoria said. "It means lady kisses. We Italians have both the lady kisses, and the *savoiardi*—the lady fingers." She grinned, and Cherie laughed.

Cherie watched Valoria work and considered the bad luck that led to the good fortune of meeting her. After helping Valoria load her pastries into the car, Cherie watched her drive away to make deliveries. Before dressing, she sent another email to Nolita telling her about finding a room to rent and asking what went wrong and if all was well. Cherie was upset but wanted to give Nolita the benefit of the doubt. She knew things happened. She didn't want to act like a bitch only to find out something happened to Nolita or that she had a reasonable excuse.

❧❧❧❧

As she filled orders for coffee, pastries, and other small bites, Valoria looked up and saw Cherie walk into the café and sit at a table to use her laptop. After finishing her work shift, Valoria made Cherie a cup of coffee and took it to her table.

"I'm glad you got out of the house," she said. She sat the hot drink down.

"Thank you," she said in appreciation for the coffee. "I decided to be brave and follow your instructions to the underground. I'm proud of myself. I bought tickets, figured out the line I needed, and found my way here."

"Did you hear from your friend?"

Cherie shook her head. "No, I just don't understand what happened. We had talked the night before I was to fly out. I'm worried." She sipped her coffee and tried to hide the embarrassment she was feeling over the whole situation.

Valoria could see the topic was difficult, so she changed the subject. "My shift is over. Do you want me to show you around Milan?"

"That sounds nice. I might as well see the city while I'm here."

Valoria led Cherie to her car then drove to Sempione Park where they took a walk enjoying the pleasant day. "Over there is the tower," said Valoria. "If you'd like we can go see the aquarium before you leave."

"That sounds nice," Cherie said softly.

Valoria noticed that Cherie had become quiet. She could not imagine being in an unfamiliar place with the one person she depended on, disappearing.

"If you want to shop you should do it during the week. The weekend will be chaotic."

"I'm wondering if I should just see if I can get an early flight home. I feel like I'm taking advantage of you and your time. It's not like you were prepared to take in a stranger and play tour guide."

"It's fine," said Valoria. "Let's sit there."

She walked to a shaded bench and sat down. Cherie sat next to her with a heavy sigh.

"I'm sorry Italy has been a bad experience, and your friend has not contacted you."

"I'm such a fool," Cherie said.

"It's a shame you don't have her new address. I looked up Nolita Barese, and I didn't find anything definitive."

"Yeah, I looked her up too. I didn't even find her name listed for her old address. It was some woman by the name of Gianna something. I mailed some items to a post box, but that won't help." Cherie sat back on the bench.

"We could go to the old address or wait at the post office and see what happens."

"Thanks, but I don't want to involve you in a possible confrontation." Cherie looked at Valoria and tried to smile. "Even if I find her I don't know what excuse she could give me that would make what she's done acceptable."

"She could be dead."

"Don't say that!" Cherie slapped Valoria's leg.

Valoria chuckled. "It could be that she is just not

a true friend."

"I guess." Cherie considered telling Valoria the truth about the friendship between her and Nolita. Valoria might kick her out, and if that happened, she could just buy an early flight home. Trying to be casual, she hesitantly looked over at Valoria.

"I thought she was more than a friend," she said softly. Valoria did not react so she continued. "I thought we were in a relationship. I've known her for a year. I believed I loved her. I mean, I think I do...love her."

Valoria guessed that was the case. Not many people cried at night over just a friend standing them up, but a love interest she understood. Meeting a lover in person for the first time was much more stressful than meeting a friend.

"Maybe she thinks you won't love her if you meet."

"Maybe." Cherie was relieved Valoria took the news well. "But, I've seen her face." She hesitated, blushing a little. "I've seen more than her face. That's why I came."

"You wanted more than just to look."

"Yes."

"What are you going to do if she doesn't meet you while you're here and she tries to talk to you again once you're home?"

Cherie ran her hand over her hair. "I'm not sure."

"Well, I think she is the one who is foolish for not meeting you."

"Thank you." Cherie blushed again.

"If you'd like, I can take you to the gay bars this weekend. We have a few good ones."

Cherie looked at her in surprise. "You go to gay

bars?"

Valoria laughed. "I let that slip, didn't I?"

"I'm pretty quick." Cherie laughed.

"Well, it's only fair since you came out to me about your situation." She gave a small smile. "I bought a two bedroom house because my girlfriend and I moved in together. As you can see, it didn't work out."

"Then you probably understand more than I thought you would." Cherie thought it was too bad she had not come to Italy to see Valoria, even if for a friendship and not romantic. She knew her thoughts were a betrayal of the relationship she had with Nolita, but the situation made her angry.

"I do. But I think you should make the best of the situation. You're in the greatest country in the world for wine, food, and amore. Focus on the things you can control and not the people you can't. You never know, maybe this girl will make an appearance before you leave and things will work out."

⁂

Cherie took Valoria's advice to enjoy her Italian vacation. She did tours, shopped and tried the local cuisine while Valoria was at work. Evenings were spent preparing recipes from her gourmet food truck menu for Valoria to try. Cherie had been nervous but Valoria enjoyed her cooking, and that gave her the confidence to continue the special dinners. She loved to cook, and she enjoyed having someone around who appreciated the food.

"Honey, I'm home," Valoria called in a singsong voice then laughed because having someone home cooking her dinner was such a novelty. She walked into the kitchen and saw the dinner waiting on the table. "It smells good in here."

"Thank you." Cherie poured wine into their glasses. "Everything's ready when you are."

"Let me clean up then I'll be back down. Do you think you'll be in the mood for dancing and a few drinks tonight? I promised to take you to the gay bars, and this is the best night to go since I don't have to be up so early tomorrow."

Cherie could not help smiling in anticipation. "I'm game! I bought the perfect dress yesterday for dancing."

"Oh, then I better break out my good clothes, so I don't look like a poor baker!" Valoria laughed as she ran upstairs to clean up.

❧ ❧ ❧ ❧

Dinner was relaxing, and they lingered over their wine having a good conversation until it was time to get ready for a night of music and dancing. They took the underground to a station that was a short walk from the club. Valoria told her friends they would be there so after paying the cover, they found the table where they were waiting.

"Everyone, this is Cherie," Valoria said repeating herself in Italian and telling them to be nice.

"Ciao," several said as they took in the woman their friend brought to the club.

Cherie could feel the judgment but stood her ground. She was not Valoria's girlfriend, so she had nothing to prove. As Valoria spoke with her friends, Cherie looked around the club taking in the crowd and the music.

"Let's get drinks," said Valoria into Cherie's ear then pulled her to the bar. "You have to excuse my friends. They think I'm crazy for renting my house to a stranger. After a few drinks, they'll be won over."

"Then I'll buy the first round," Cherie said with a smile.

As predicted, Valoria's friends were happy to have a round of drinks provided. Everyone took up their shots, shouted "*alla goccia*," and then downed them. After a few drinks, everyone seemed to be more relaxed. Valoria translated when needed, but most of her friends knew some English, especially those who worked with tourists. The crowd in the club got larger, as the dance floor filled up with more people. Soon they were all out dancing.

Cherie's dress was perfect for dancing and Valoria was a great dance partner who knew a lot of different dances and led very well. The teasing by her friends was all in good fun, and Valoria insisted that they were jealous. They were enjoying their drinks and the energy in the club. The dancing became a free for all with a cross between real dance moves and jumping up and down.

Grabbing Valoria's arm to get her attention, Cherie motioned to the bar and said, "I need some water, and I'm thirsty and exhausted!"

"All right." Valoria followed Cherie and slammed into her back as Cherie stopped in her tracks. "What are you doing?"

Cherie pointed across the dance floor. "I think that's her. I think that's Nolita!"

She looked at Valoria with shock showing on her face. She had been emailing her every day without a reply. If Nolita was in the city and going out dancing, it meant that no tragedy had happened. All this time she had been so close yet refused to return an email or call. She was not sure what to do. She was overwhelmed with hurt and confusion.

"Do you want to talk to her?" Valoria waited for an answer. Cherie just stood in place. "Cherie, what do you want to do? Are you sure it's her?"

Watching Nolita out on the dance floor grinding on and kissing the woman she was obviously with, left a sick feeling inside Cherie. She was not sure if she wanted to talk with her. Talking might crack the fragile shell of indifference she built over the past week. If it broke, she knew that talking would be impossible through the inevitable tears. That was the woman she came to see and who she knew intimately. The person she was so sure she was in love with even though they had only corresponded via technology.

Cherie leaned heavily onto Valoria's arm because her legs were weakening.

"I don't know what to do." She looked at Valoria in desperation. "She obviously doesn't want any contact with me. She probably thinks I'm sitting somewhere pining over her."

She was sure that was where she would be if not for Valoria.

Valoria's friends had noticed something amiss and had gathered around. Valoria quickly gave a summary of everything in Italian. Her friends stared at Nolita outraged.

"I'm going over," said Valoria. "I'll just talk to her nicely and see if she will explain herself." She motioned to her friend to take Cherie's arm then made her way to Nolita.

"Valoria is, uh, *cazzuta*," said one of the girls.

"Woman with the balls. She will fix things for you. This *figa scianca* will be sorry."

Valoria returned with Nolita and the woman she was with. Nolita looked at her with what Cherie could only describe as contempt...contempt from the woman who told her that she loved her almost every day for a year. The same woman Cherie had shared her intimate secrets. Who she'd given everything, except her physical self. The woman she had intended to give her heart, soul, and body. Cherie felt weak, like a fool, and sick to her stomach.

"Cherie." Valoria saw her turning pale and tried to take her arm.

"No," said Cherie. She avoided Valoria's touch because her resolve might break and she would lose herself to tears. She looked at Nolita and could barely breathe. "Why?"

Nolita stayed silent, but the woman with her did not. She was speaking quickly and angrily in Italian. All Cherie could do was wait for an answer.

"She's asking her who you are," said Valoria. "She is her girlfriend."

Cherie's illusion shattered even more, and she could not stop her body from shaking in pain.

"It was just something to do." Nolita shrugged. "I did you a favor by talking to you. I didn't think you would come here."

"You knew. We talked."

"Why didn't you answer her emails?" asked Valoria crossing her arms.

"I don't know." Nolita shrugged again. "I never expected to see you."

"That's not what you said to me. You told me you loved me and wanted to be with me." Cherie's head was spinning, and the world seemed skewed.

Valoria said something in Italian and Nolita and her girlfriend started arguing.

"I told her what you said, and now she's angry at Nolita too." Valoria wasn't sure if she should tell her all the things Nolita was saying about her. It might make the pain showing on Cherie's face worse.

"You should go home and don't contact me again," Nolita said abruptly. "I only love Gianna."

Nolita's declaration hit Cherie like a physical blow. She felt herself almost fall, but Valoria held onto her.

"I need to go," Cherie said so softly that Valoria barely heard it under the loud music. She pulled away from Valoria's hold and staggered toward the door.

Valoria watched her push through the crowd then turned her anger onto Nolita.

"You are sick! How could you do that to someone?" She looked at Gianna. "This is who you are with, a person that causes pain in others for no reason. Your girlfriend told that girl," she pointed in the direction Cherie had gone, "that she loved her every day for almost a year. She played with her heart and emotions."

"It was her fault for believing me," said Nolita defensively. "It was a game, and she thought it was real! She is stupid."

"It wasn't a game to her," Valoria said evenly. "She told me all about you."

Nolita shrugged again. "I gave her what she wanted. She should be grateful I was so nice."

The shrugging pissed Valoria off.

"You are disgusting and insane. Cherie is a lovely woman. She doesn't deserve this misleading treatment." She watched Nolita shrug again then she looked at Gianna. "I hope she doesn't treat you this way."

"She doesn't," Gianna snapped. "She loves me."

"You sound very sure," said Valoria evenly. "I wonder how many others she's telling she loves every day besides Cherie. If she gives her love away so cheaply, what is her love for you worth?"

"Come, Valoria," said one of her friends. "You should go find Cherie."

Valoria wanted to punch Nolita but knew it would only escalate the problem and possibly keep her from getting to Cherie.

"I hope we never run into each other again." Valoria turned and walked away.

"Fuck you!" Nolita shouted over the music. "She's just a dumb bitch!"

Valoria did not turn around but heard a commotion and knew one of her friends had punched Nolita. At least someone got to release her anger. She hurried out of the club then ran to try and catch Cherie.

℣℣℣

Valoria rushed into her house in a panic. She had not found Cherie and hoped she was home. As she climbed the stairs, she could hear Cherie crying. Relief flooded her that she was safe. She opened the bedroom door quietly and found Cherie on the bed. Her heart went out to her, and she climbed onto the bed taking her into her arms.

"I'm so sorry," Valoria said softly.

"I'm such a fool," she sobbed.

"No," Valoria assured her. "You're just a

romantic. We romantics get in trouble like this a lot it seems."

"It hurts," Cherie said through her tears.

"I know."

"I guess I deserve it for giving my heart to a stranger."

"No one deserves to be hurt like this." She pulled Cherie closer. "I think Jako punched her if that helps."

"She did?" In a way, it helped. In another way it just made her feel even more like a fool that someone had to come to her rescue.

"It was either her or Brina, but I think it's more like Jako to throw a punch."

"I hope they don't get into trouble."

"They'll be fine."

They lay together for a while as Cherie cried off and on. Soon she was cried out.

"You must think I'm a mess," said Cherie after taking a deep shuddering breath and letting it out.

"You are a mess." Valoria smiled when Cherie reached back and slapped her leg. "I mean sometimes love is messy."

Cherie gave a short laugh. "Apparently." She moved away from Valoria's embrace and turned over to look at her. "Thank you for being so kind. I can't imagine what you think of me. I invade your job, your house, and cause a scene. You must think I'm pathetic."

Valoria looked into Cherie's puffy eyes then turned onto her back. "I don't." She turned and looked at her again. "The first time I looked at you I thought, that woman has a lot of luggage." She chuckled as Cherie sighed. "The second time I looked at you I thought, for her size, that woman is taking up a lot of space." This time Cherie laughed out loud. "Then when I talked to you my heart said, keep this woman safe, help her, she is good. That's why I offered you a place to stay. My heart was right."

"Do you always listen to your heart?"

"No," she said softly. She turned her body to face Cherie. "My heart has been telling me to kiss you since I met you. I didn't because you seemed so in love with someone else." Cherie looked at her and said nothing. "Now, I wish I would have listened. Latin hearts are rarely wrong about these things. Maybe, if I'd have listened to my heart, you wouldn't have been so hurt tonight." She moved closer and gently placed her lips on Cherie's. She felt Cherie's passion as she pulled her close and kissed her deeper.

"Wait," said Cherie pulling away, catching her breath and fighting to calm her heart. "I'm not sure I can do this now."

"I'm sorry." Stung, Valoria sat up thinking it might be best that she leave.

Cherie put her hand on her arm. "Don't go." She waited for Valoria to lie back down. "It's just. I've been through an emotional ringer tonight. I don't want either of us doing anything that we might regret or cause more pain."

"Okay," said Valoria nodding her agreement. She gathered Cherie back into her arms and kissed her forehead. "I'm here for you."

Cherie closed her eyes and felt comfort and warmth flow through her in response to Valoria's kiss. Her mind was full of conflicting thoughts, some leading toward pain and others to Valoria. She did not want to confuse any real feelings she might have for Valoria with the need to feel comfort and support. That would only lead to pain for them both.

"Cherie?"

"Yeah."

"Would you like some lady kisses?"

Cherie couldn't help laughing. "You mean the cookies?"

"Maybe both kinds of lady kisses? When you're ready."

Looking at Valoria's grin, Cherie's heart melted. "I think I'd like them both."

"Just wait until I give you my lady fingers." She chuckled as Cherie slapped her lightly on the shoulder.

"I'm glad you listened to your heart."

C. L. Cattano is an independent author, artist, and seeker of whimsy. Her first book was Cursed Hearts. Her current project is the new serial Salvaggio's Light and the first book, Shattered Paradise, released March 2017. Cattano lives in the Midwest with her partner and their dog, Bella.

The Girl on the Bus

By Maria Siopis

Alexia felt her blood boiling beneath her skin. Surprisingly, this was something entirely different than what she had experienced her whole life. It wasn't like an electric current that traveled through her body and then subsided. It felt like heat. She was certain of it. She turned to look at the person behind her who crashed into her accidentally when the bus stopped short. She wanted to smile at the girl, but she got nervous as soon as she gazed at her eyes. She somehow found her wording and whispered her regret for hurting her, although it wasn't Alexia's fault. The girl touched her arm to reassure her that she was okay. She felt it again. Her blood was surging within her, creating heat waves.

Alexia knew the girl as she saw her at the bus stop every morning. She liked her, and she was attracted to her, but she was hesitant to speak to her. Knowing her face well, if asked, Alexia could draw it with precision. Trying not to be obvious she observed the girl's face for a few seconds at a time. Not because she was shy, she liked her, and that made her nervous.

Time rolled by and for a whole year Alexia fantasized about the girl on the bus constructing imaginary scenarios about her life. Sometimes the plot took a different turn, and she found herself caressing the girl's body. On these occasions, Alexia came sooner than intended but it was epically enjoyable at the moment. Nevertheless, she felt ashamed and guilty about her fantasies when she saw the girl standing at the bus stop. Perhaps that was the reason she didn't approach her. She felt guilty taking advantage of the girl in her make-believe-world and her sexual fantasies.

This morning, after the girl's body slammed into hers, Alexia's protected fantasy world shattered into a thousand pieces. She knew she couldn't go on pretending the feelings that were brewing inside were just an attraction she could control. She realized it was bigger than that. She had confirmation. The girl made her blood boil and uncontrollably race through her veins.

"I'm Alexia by the way," she said and extended her hand. Where did she find the courage?

"Cara," she replied.

Alexia held the girl's hand for just a nanosecond, yet she felt the softness. She desired to kiss it at that moment. Her lips parted a bit. *Fuck*, her inner voice screamed. She looked down instead to gather her thoughts before she said or did something stupid or objectionable.

"Well, I'm sorry again," said Alexia.

"I should be sorry for almost taking you down to a fall." Cara smiled, and Alexia felt a tingle between her legs.

The bus came to a full stop, and Alexia turned and walked the narrow alley between the seats holding her purse in front of her. She thanked the bus driver as she did every day and exited without looking back at Cara. Flustered, her face felt burning hot. She had a bad feeling about this encounter. She wanted to create distance for now. She had to calm the fuck down and think. What just happened between them? She was attracted to Cara for a year. She had fantasies about her, and their accidental touch created emotional havoc within her.

There were other issues to consider. What if Cara was straight or in a relationship? Deep inside she wished that none of it were true. Trying not to ponder upon the incident, her attempts to forget the girl with the big eyelashes and broad smile, failed. She thought about her more than once at work and concentrating on legal matters became impossible.

She sighed with relief when she left the office as she could now let her mind consider Cara without the distraction of work. Was she obsessing over her? Perhaps she should change her schedule and avoid her until she figured out what it was about the girl on the bus. She was striking with the bluest eyes she'd ever seen on a person. Alexia could easily penetrate Cara's soul if she could only let herself wander in Cara's eyes. Cara's blond curly hair usually wild and unmanageable added to her charm. Alexia thought about making love to her as her hand mingled with the mass of Cara's hair pulling her closer to her lips and kissing her deeply.

She was wet from these thoughts and cursed under her breath. She didn't want to consider Cara as her mate yet. At night when she was under her covers she let her hand traverse her body and touch her softness. Cara was there, and she felt the warm body next to hers sharing this intimate moment. It took a second for Alexia to come. As she closed her eyes Cara's smiling face appeared in front of her guiding her to the dark and quiet world of non-existence.

Alexia clenched her purse as soon as she saw Cara approaching. She was nervous to talk to her particularly after their unintentional touch on the bus and the fantasies she had about Cara the night before. She looked down to avoid the awkward moment, but all was forgotten when Cara touched her arm to get her attention.

"Oh hi," Alexia said as if she was surprised by her presence there. "Are you okay?" She inquired.

"Good morning," she replied cheerfully. "I'm okay. Thank you."

This simple interaction was the beginning of a relationship that made Alexia happy and content more than any other time. She was in love with Cara and questioned her feelings. Was it even possible to love someone so quickly? Or was it that lesbian thing that abstracted her better judgment? Where everything happened fast and died faster? She didn't consider the latter because the feelings she had for Cara felt real.

She recalled their first date and smiled as her gaze fell upon the document she was studying. She was thankful that Cara asked her out because she didn't have the guts to do it herself. How did she know? Perhaps it was more obvious than Alexia thought. It only took a glance and a simple touch to know if there was an interest. They both agreed there was electricity flowing freely between them. It felt like destiny.

Alexia closed her file and got up. She was already late, and she didn't want Cara arriving at her dwelling before she did.

Her commute was quick, and she made it with

a few minutes to spare before Cara arrived. They embraced hard and kissed as if it was the first time. Alexia hovered over Cara's mouth savoring her scent as her hands worked on taking off Cara's shirt. She tried to be patient while undoing the buttons, but she gave up and ripped it off of Cara's body. She kissed Cara's collarbone continuing to her breast covered by a white lace bra.

"Baby, I'm crazy about you," Alexia whispered as she removed the white bra and let Cara's breast free. She brushed Cara's exposed skin with her lips and closed her eyes thinking about their intense connection, sexually and otherwise. She moaned as her mouth engulfed Cara's nipple while she unzipped her pants.

"Babe, time out, time out," Cara mumbled out of breath. "If you don't stop I'll come right here by this door."

Alexia smiled as if she found her utterance amusing.

"That's the point," she replied and ignored her.

When Cara's orgasm erupted, Alexia was between her legs with her face buried deep into her irresistible center. She kissed her way up to Cara's lips and then took her hand into hers guiding her into the bedroom. She had just gotten started.

"Babe, I have to talk to you," Cara said looking in her eyes adoringly. Or that was how Alexia interpreted it after their sexual thirst was a bit satisfied.

"I'm relocating," she whispered, "for work."

"Where?"

Cara didn't answer. She remained silent for a while, and she appeared to be contemplating on how to continue. Alexia panicked. Life without Cara was unimaginable. She became accustomed to seeing her in her apartment after work, eating dinner with her, watching TV, and sometimes she stayed over. The last year was the best part of her entire life other than practicing law. She waited patiently for Cara to reply. In her mind, she wanted to know instantly.

"Well?"

"It's another country," Cara finally articulated.

"Fuck. Seriously?"

"Baby, we can do this."

"Yeah. How? These types of relationships never last."

"We love each other."

It was Alexia's turn to remain silent, and not because she didn't have anything to say. She stopped talking to shift through her thoughts. This woman who was next to her lying in bed meant more than any other she had met in the past. She would do anything to keep her in her arms.

"Stay with me."

"Alexia, I have to do it. I love my job. It's cathartic and fulfilling."

Cara never addressed her by name before except early in their relationship. This was serious.

"I noticed you from the very beginning," Alexia said instead. "For an entire year, I fantasized having you in my arms. I felt tortured with the idea of you being in a relationship or even being straight. I love you. I think I loved you from that first day."

"Babe, I love you too but understand that this is big. I'll be in charge of a hospital. I'll help people, kids, and adults alike. Save lives that matter."

"I'm afraid to ask where specifically in the world."

"Afghanistan. It's going to be safe I'll be inside

an American base."

"Right in the war zone. It doesn't mean anything. The American base is still a target." Alexia felt broken into tiny insignificant and worthless pieces. What could she do to keep her girlfriend here without jeopardizing her career or needs?

"I don't think I can do it. I just can't bear the thought of being away from you or the worrying for you every time the news comes on."

"So are you going to let go of our relationship? Is that what you want?" Cara said.

Alexia desired to keep her sheltered and protected from any harm, but she also knew her girlfriend was strong willed and the need to help others was greater than her own needs. At the same time, after many years in the dating scene, Alexia had already experienced the ending of a long distance relationship more than once.

"I'll wait for you," Alexia finally uttered as she took Cara in her arms and kissed her until her lips were sore. She was willing to try one more time.

ᘓᘒᘓᘒ

Alexia had done some crazy things in her life, but the latest was the most elaborate of all. She closed her eyes as she rested her head on the seat of the plane with her seatbelt fastened recalling what brought her to the current situation. It was love, of course. She loved this woman who was at the other end of the world, and she was going to see her. The last five months were not as smooth as she hoped because every single day she missed Cara more. She hadn't talked to her girlfriend for over a month because she didn't want to spoil the surprise of her visit. She knew that would appear suspicious since they spoke weekly, but she took the chance. And besides, she worked too hard for this trip. Persuading her friend, General Frank Sabatico, to assist her in reaching the American base in Afghanistan in one piece wasn't an easy task. She presented her argument to him, and although she was a compelling litigator, Frank appeared untouched until she told him that she wanted to propose to Cara. Frank smiled widely and took her in his arms promising that he would make the trip happen. She didn't feel a bit guilty for lying to him. She had purchased the ring afterward as the idea made perfect sense to her. There was nothing else to consider other than her love for Cara. She hoped that she would accept the proposal to be her wife.

She wished to go to sleep, but her anxiety was taking over. No matter how hard she tried, she remained wide-awake. The engines of the plane were louder than a commercial airliner, disturbing her further. She opened her eyes and looked around to the faces of the men and women that took the oath to protect their country and admiration filled her heart. Even Cara's Hippocratic oath filled her insides with feelings of pride and honor. She smiled as she acknowledged her girlfriend was a fighter who safeguarded the well being of people.

The flight was uncomfortable and long, with the connecting flight through Germany. The captain assured her that they had reached the midpoint and the flight time to the air base in Kabul from Frankfurt would be seven hours and forty minutes. Alexia settled down once again thinking that love was ironic and made people do uncharacteristic things. She never expected that she would visit an air base in a dangerous country for the sake of love.

When she first saw the air base from above, it was not what she expected. She had visualized identical barracks surrounded by fences along the perimeters, but there weren't any fences. Instead, there was uniform housing, a large number of parked military planes, dirt roads, expansive flatlands, and mountains surrounding the perimeters. How did they secure this place? She wondered. She tried to pinpoint the hospital, but it was impossible since there were no special signs.

"The one with the flags," the young woman sitting next to her said as if she knew what Alexia was thinking. Her heart danced in her chest.

She became nervous again as soon as they landed. She couldn't contain her urgency to glimpse Cara's delicate face. She would go to the end of the world for her, she was certain. Hell, she was at the end of the world. She was dropped off at the hospital and progressed toward the entrance pulling the luggage behind her. She looked like a tourist who got lost. When she heard the sounds of an unidentifiable object flying over her head and the explosion, she knew for a fact that she didn't belong here. She instinctively covered her ears and closed her eyes. She turned around, but no one appeared shaken or even acknowledged the fact that a missile exploded. She quickened her pace and stopped the first person she met to inquire about Cara. The nurse, a beautiful woman in her thirties, looked at her inquisitively but guided her to Cara's office.

"I'll take it from here," Alexia said to her.

The nurse reluctantly left her in front of the closed door but turned to watch Alexia again, carefully observing. Alexia forgot all about the nurse as soon as she opened the door to face the only person that mattered in her life. Cara's gaze met hers.

❧ ❧ ❧ ❧

Time is going forward, only forward, Alexia thought as she glanced at her watch. She hadn't been at work early for the longest time, but lately, she didn't give a fuck. The happy moments of her job were gone, and nothing could change that. Today for an unknown reason Alexia woke up early. She got ready quickly because she wanted to make the first bus the way she used to do eons ago before Cara happened. A bitter smile reached her lips. How could she have been so stupid and not read between the lines? She felt that something was wrong, but she ignored her intuition and the nurse that had greeted her on the air base. Cara's betrayal became agonizingly painful because the nurse, she wouldn't use her name, told her about the affair. If Cara came to her first, perhaps she would be able to forgive her. She was an idiot to consider it. Cara wasn't worthy of her attention and feelings.

Alexia wanted to turn back time or even erase the past with a brush and paint like an artist creating a different scene where the nurse never existed. She would paint the base and the hospital and her proposing to Cara. What was the point of recalling the past? Their relationship had unexpectedly dissolved. Her girlfriend apologized to no avail as Alexia had made up her mind. She couldn't forgive her.

"You don't know how it is here. You haven't called me in a month." Cara accused her when the details of the affair surfaced.

"And that gives you the right to sleep around?" Alexia came back with her remark. "I wanted to surprise you."

Alexia left the hospital without giving Cara the opportunity to defend her actions, and she was regretting it now. Two and a half months had passed from that dreadful day. Still, it remained crystal clear in Alexia's mind. She wondered why Cara didn't stop her from leaving. Was she in love with the nurse?

She glanced at the clock again and grabbed her purse, urgently exiting her apartment to reach that first bus. She felt the light breeze caressing her face and inhaled filling her lungs with fresh air. She walked, passing tall buildings with architecture identical to the base in Afghanistan. *What is it with me recalling the shattered past?* She wondered. The bus stop was surprisingly empty, but she didn't mind a bit. Her gaze fell to the ground noticing the minuscule creatures, the ants that moved continuously. She got lost in her thoughts again.

It was logical for Alexia to jump when she felt a touch on her arm. Did her face appear surprised or did it show her panic? She needed a few minutes to calm the fuck down.

"Hi," she finally said. "What are you doing here?"

"I'm back," Cara answered, and Alexia detected a sad smile on her face. "I never stopped thinking about you."

Alexia was incapable of processing what was unfolding in front of her. What was she supposed to say when her heart had made up its own decision and her mind was full of logic? Cara had lost weight, and her cheekbones protruded underneath her skin. She was still pretty, but a few extra pounds would have made her irresistible. Alexia was biased, and no matter how Cara appeared she would always see her as a mortal goddess. They boarded the bus and sat next to each other. Cara took her hand into hers and Alexia didn't protest. It felt familiar and warm.

"Can we talk?" Cara ventured.

Alexia kissed her cheek and then reached into her purse to recover the jewelry box she had nested in the side pocket for more than two months.

"I came to Afghanistan to give you this. I kept it in my purse all this time."

Cara opened the box and tears formed at the edge of her blue oceans.

"I hurt you. I hope you forgive me. I'm miserable without you. I love you. I almost died in Afghanistan, and Rose was there supporting me and caring about me. I was exposed and alone. I wasn't in love with her, and I regret getting involved. I'm not trying to excuse my behavior, but being out there in the war zone is different. You wake up and go to sleep thinking about death. I'm disappointed with myself for hurting you."

"Don't be. Life is strange. I love you, and always will. I can't put all this behind me. I'll think about you and hurt for a long while." She stopped, swallowing the lump that gathered at her throat and continued. "I want you to keep the ring, it's yours," she said as she got up.

Alexia's stop was approaching. She kissed Cara's cheek again and exited the bus with the heaviest heart. Long distance relationships never worked, she thought as she crossed the street. She was surprised with herself, how composed she appeared in front of Cara yet her insides were collapsing at a fast pace. Her teary eyes abstracted her vision, but she kept going forward.

Maria Siopis possesses an MPA in Emergency Management and Homeland Security. She completed her dissertation, "Avian Influenza (H5N1): The Doctrine of Social Disassociation, Quarantine, and Emergency Preparedness," in 2006 tackling a non-fictional theme. Other than writing she obsesses over climatic or manmade catastrophes and continuously attempts to conceptualize needed actions. The author lives in New York and is currently working on her second novel.

Chat Room Rescue

By Shiloh Saddler

Elise had graduated with a business degree, but she didn't want to work for someone else. She wanted to run her own company. Ever since high school, Elise had a dream, a mission. She'd learned about other parts of the world where gay and lesbian people were persecuted and prosecuted. Being lesbian she hated the thought of people living in fear or hiding their preferences and lovers. Four years ago she'd founded the Green Light International Travel Agency. The agency, besides the usual travel business, helped the GLBT communities in other non-accepting countries visit and relocate to a more accepting nation. Now that gay and lesbian couples were allowed to marry in the United States, more people were requesting to travel here.

This morning she entered the office early before any of her employees. She sipped her Starbucks mocha while turning on her computer. Clicking over to her website she typed in the private URL. It opened her secret chat room. One of her college buddies, Brent, a government tech specialist, had designed her website ensuring the chat room was as secure as Fort Knox. He understood the dire consequences that could result from someone hacking into their chat room where

GLBT people corresponded with each other. Similar to an old-fashioned matchmaking service, once a couple agreed to meet each other she'd arrange the travel plan. Sometimes couples couldn't afford the ticket, and she'd use profits from the agency to cover it. Green Light gained more of the travel agency business each year, and there were a lot of people en route out of New York. The arranged partnerships didn't always work out, but she took pride in all the success stories.

She sipped her coffee and glanced through the incoming messages sent to the chat moderator. Keeping the chat room running was more labor intensive than orchestrating the necessary paperwork for arranging the travel. She spent most of her time in the chat room while her employees handled the travel end of the business.

Her friends had started teasing her that she could find partners for other people, but couldn't find one for herself. She'd corresponded with many women but so far hadn't found the right one. For love to bloom over email or chat messages, there had to be some common ground, a connection.

In all caps, one chat member wrote in the subject line: PLEASE HELP ME

She skipped the messages above it and clicked open that one.

"My name is Adia Kamau. I live in Nairobi, Kenya. I must get out of the country as soon as possible. I will go anywhere. My father found out that I prefer women. He said that if he ever saw me again, he'd kill me. I believe him. Please help. You're my only hope for a future."

Elise stared at the desperate message. Nothing this severe had come across the chat room before. A chill slithered down her back until her whole body numbed. She knew she had to help Adia.

"I'm sorry to hear of your situation. Of course, I will help. I will get my people started on paperwork right away. You will need to give me more personal details. Do you have a passport?"

Elise drummed her fingers on the top of her desk. It took weeks to get a passport. She prayed that Adia already had one. Staring at the computer and waiting for a reply was as bad as watching a pot full of water and waiting for it to boil. She sighed and strolled around the small office. The ticking of the large white clock on the wall rang in her ears. Her nerves frayed by the second until she almost ripped the batteries out of the clock to make it stop ticking.

Ding. Adia had replied. She raced to her chair and sat down so fast that she spun around. She grabbed the edge of the desk and pulled herself around to face the computer screen.

"Yes. I have a passport. I have traveled before, but not to the U.S."

Elise exhaled the breath she hadn't realized she'd been holding. She didn't know this woman at all, yet she felt a strong connection with her, and need to protect her. She got that way with all her lovers. That's what had ended her last relationship. The woman said she felt smothered, that Elise had hovered too close. Maybe Adia wouldn't mind. Elise tried to curb her deeply ingrained habits. It was impossible.

"That's great. You will travel to the United States. I live in a small apartment in New York City. There is room enough for two."

The office door opened with a loud squeak. Elise jumped out of her chair.

"I didn't mean to startle you," Trisha said. "Is something wrong?"

"I was deep in thought."

"I could see that."

Deciding to keep Adia's situation private, Elise decided to build a story.

"I'm waiting to get more details from a woman in Nairobi. She is coming to live in New York City."

Trisha nodded. "As soon as you get all the details I'll get right on it. Coming to live here, huh? Who is the lucky woman? Anyone, we know?"

"New York is a big city," Elise hedged.

"Yes...but we are quite involved in the lesbian community."

Elise smiled. She knew she couldn't keep it a secret for long. Trisha would badger her with questions. "Yes, it is someone we know."

Trisha rubbed her palms together. "Who?"

Elise glanced away and whispered, "She's coming to live with me."

"You?" Trisha exclaimed. "You never told us anything! You've been corresponding with a woman, and you didn't let us know?" Her tone contained false hurt. The gleam in Trisha's sapphire eyes let her know how much her friend was happy for her.

If it wasn't for the three-inch heels, Trisha insisted on wearing Elise imagined she'd be jumping up and down. The curvy woman could be a plus size model, and she didn't mind flaunting it.

"I'm bringing Adia to the United States to escape persecution, not as my lover."

Trisha quirked a brow but nodded her agreement.

"Okay. Well, we will make sure to give Adia a warm welcome. As soon as John gets here, we'll start planning a party."

"Party?" Elise squeaked. She didn't want to scare the woman away the minute she arrived. "I'm not sure that's a good idea."

"Don't be silly. Of course, it's a good idea. Adia will have to meet your crazy friends if she's living with you. You can't hide us forever."

Elise rolled her eyes. She didn't believe she could keep her best friend Trisha away for five minutes. The woman was always in the middle of everything. John loved to plan a good party as much as Trisha did. Once those two got together, nothing could stop them. And Adia might even see fireworks exploding off their apartment veranda if John could wrangle the permit.

As if on cue, John entered the office in his usual polo shirt, forest green this time to bring out his eyes and tailored khaki slacks. Her two employees dressed up even if they claimed they only wore business casual. Should she buy a new outfit for meeting Adia? None of her clothes did anything to help her stocky figure.

"Guess what?" Trisha asked, running over to John before Elise could stop her. "You'll never guess."

John blew out a breath.

"You got that miniature poodle you've been talking about?"

"No."

"You found me a cheaper apartment?"

Trisha laughed. "No."

John shrugged. "I give. What is it?"

"Elise found a woman!"

John's eyes widened. "Tell me about her. Where did you meet?"

"See this is why I waited to tell you guys," Elise said. "Too many questions."

"Too many questions? We haven't even gotten started yet," John said in a snappy tone.

"She met her through the agency's chat room," Trisha said. "Her name is Adia."

"And she's from Nairobi, Kenya," Elise added not wanting Trisha to say everything.

She knew that her two friends would have a lot more questions than she could answer. They just had to take this one step at a time.

Her computer dinged. She swiveled in her computer chair back to face the monitor.

"Adia gave me all the details we need to organize her travel."

She pulled a pen and piece of paper out of her desk drawer, wrote down all the details and handed it to Trisha. She wished that Adia could be on the next flight to the United States. Even with a passport, organizing everything would take a few days.

"Is there a place you are staying?"

Adia hadn't mentioned that in her last message. "No."

No? What did no mean? Elise thought while taking slow deep breaths to keep from freaking out.

"You have to stay somewhere. How can I remain in contact with you?"

"I'm out on the street. I borrow a computer. I will stay in touch as much as I can."

Elise gulped. She knew how rough it was for the homeless in New York City, imagining it would be just as bad if not worse for the homeless in Nairobi. She couldn't get Adia to the United States fast enough. She had another question to ask.

"How did your father find out you are a lesbian?"

Was she leaving a lover in Kenya? Elise realized

that she would do anything to ensure her safety, but if she had feelings for someone else those feelings won't immediately disappear. She needed to know if there was another woman at risk. If so, she'd do everything in her power to get that woman to New York City, too.

"My former best friend told him."

Whoever this friend was, she wanted to slug them. However, Adia's misfortune could work out for the best. Think positive. Elise could chat with Adia when possible. She could ask her questions, get to know her. She had a lot to share and discuss with a new roommate. Trisha and John were capable of running the travel agency. At least when Adia was on her computer, Elise would know she was safe. Now, Elise didn't know if she'd get much sleep until the woman arrived at the airport. It felt like they'd formed an instant connection. It was hard to believe, but the connection was there.

"I look forward to meeting you, Adia."

⁂

Elise stood at the JFK Airport with a big cardboard sign that said Adia Kamau. She'd learned that Adia had three brothers and that she was the youngest in the family. It must be hard leaving all her family and friends. Being disowned didn't make the separation any easier. Elise hoped she could find a way to ease the gaping hole in Adia's heart.

She had no idea how to recognize Adia. They hadn't discussed appearances in their limited chats. Adia completed a formal education. Her father was a dentist and the money he made put all of the children through school. Knowing she could read and write

English would simplify getting help for Adia.

Elise pulled out her cell phone to check the time. The airport arrivals board indicated Adia's flight would be landing any minute. To Elise's surprise, her heart raced at the thought of finally meeting Adia. She did not know if there would be a spark between them. She could introduce her to lots of single friends if there wasn't. They'd start the paperwork to get Adia a visa. Hopefully down the road, she could apply for citizenship.

A slender dark skinned woman timidly approached. Her straight black hair fell to her shoulders, and her casual outfit of a long white skirt paired with a tight fitting bright pink T-shirt sent Elise's temperature rising. The woman didn't wear any makeup aside from pink lipstick that matched her T-shirt.

"Are you Elise Granger?" the woman asked. She didn't have any luggage with her and Elise realized that she'd fled Nairobi without any belongings.

"Yes, I am." She dropped the cardboard sign and flung her arms around the woman, holding her close.

Adia melted into her embrace and sobbed on her shoulder.

Elise didn't have any words to make the pain go away. She stroked Adia's hair. How could a woman so young and beautiful, be turned away by her family?

Adia straightened and brushed the last of the tears from her eyes.

"I've been holding it together for so long. I just couldn't hold it in any longer."

"It's all right. I understand. Welcome to the United States."

Adia laughed, her eyes puffy from crying, brightened a fraction.

"I'm sure that wasn't the welcome you'd been anticipating."

"No. It was better than I hoped for."

Adia returned Elise's soft smile.

Elise motioned with her head leading Adia to the parking lot.

"My car is this way."

They started walking, and Elise reached over and took Adia's hand in hers. It felt right.

⁂

"Wow," Adia said, "you have a lovely apartment."

Elise didn't think so, but she was glad that Adia approved. All the apartments in this building looked the same, one bedroom, a small kitchen, and a small living room. She'd sleep on the sofa tonight and give Adia the bed. The woman was probably exhausted after the long flight.

"Are you hungry?" Elise asked. Her stomach grumbled. She'd been too anxious to eat lunch, and with a one-hour flight delay, it was past her usual dinnertime.

"Yes. I'm hungry."

Elise pressed her lips together. She wasn't much of a cook. Typically she lived on takeout. It didn't help that the kitchen was so small a person could barely move around in there with any pots or pans. "Do you like pizza?"

"Oh, yes. I love pizza. Pepperoni is my favorite."

"Pepperoni it is." She pulled her cell phone out of her pocket and hit the speed dial for the pizzeria around the corner. Thank goodness they stayed open until ten p.m.

In fifteen minutes the delivery guy knocked on the door. Elise opened it and smiled at Billy. She handed him the money.

"Pizza for dinner, huh?" Billy said.

The guy struggled to make conversation.

"Yes. Maybe I'll have Chinese tomorrow."

"Yeah, Chinese is a lot better than pizza." He glanced past her shoulder to Adia. "Oh, you have company."

She nodded. "Girls night. Have a good evening, Billy." She shut the door before the man could make a pass at Adia.

The large cardboard box heated Elise's fingers. She set it on the table in the living room. "Grab a slice." She opened the box, and pizza fumes filled the apartment.

"That's a lot of cheese." Adia picked up a slice, and the cheese stretched until it finally broke free.

"I buy their pizza a lot. The owner gives me extra cheese for free. If you don't like cheese that much I can tell them to stop."

She shook her head. "There is nothing wrong with cheese."

Elise found it awkward and yet comfortable with Adia in her apartment. She didn't know what to say to her, fearing she'd say the wrong thing and send the woman into a fit of tears. She hated tears. One breakdown was enough for the day.

"I've taken the day off from work tomorrow." *Because she didn't want her friends to hound her about Adia,* she thought. "We can go sightseeing. There are a lot of interesting things to see in New York."

"I'd like that. Can we see the Statue of Liberty?"

"Of course. That's at the top of the list."

To avoid feeling as if she needed to make conversation, Elise opted for a movie. Adia squealed like a little girl when she saw Elise's extensive movie collection. It filled a bookcase in the bedroom.

Adia stepped back from the bookcase and turned to her.

"I can't choose. You'll have to pick one."

Oh, the pressure! Dramas were not in the running. They didn't need anything that would make either of them cry. A romantic comedy seemed a good choice.

"This one." She slipped the DVD out, and they both returned to the living room.

Adia plopped down on the sofa acting right at home. Elise was glad she was more confident and relaxed than she had been at the airport.

"What did you pick?"

"You'll see."

Elise opened the DVD player and inserted 50 First Dates. Under the circumstances, it seemed appropriate. Could tonight be their first date? She secretly hoped it was.

They both laughed, and Adia snuggled closer to her on the sofa. Elise wrapped her arm around her shoulders, and they stayed cozy until the end of the movie.

"Are you ready for bed?" Elise asked. "I only have one bedroom. It has clean sheets. You can sleep in the bed, and I'll just stay out here. The sofa is comfortable."

"I'd hate to make you leave your room. That bed looked big enough for two."

Butterflies unleashed in Elise's stomach. She hadn't expected the invitation.

"Yes, I suppose it is. I'm warning you. I do snore."

Adia chuckled. "Well if that's your only bad habit then I think we'll manage."

Elise loved to hear her laugh.

"And I steal the covers."

Adia chuckled harder.

"Well if you steal all the covers then I'll just have to lie close to you to keep warm."

A lump sprouted in Elise's throat and she swallowed.

They each took their turn in the bathroom getting ready for bed. Elise gave Adia an extra toothbrush, and she said that was all she needed. Elise hoped that soon she'd need a lot more.

When Adia stepped out of the bathroom naked, Elise was speechless. She couldn't stop staring at her smooth skin. Her gaze traveled from the woman's pert breasts to her mound.

"I didn't realize…"

"No other clothes." Adia shrugged as if she didn't care.

"Oh. That's right. We'll have to go clothes shopping tomorrow."

Both of them lay in the full-size bed. Elise's blocky frame took up half of it, but Adia didn't seem to mind. Elise lay on her back staring up at the ceiling. Her heart raced, and the need to touch Adia rode her hard. If she rolled over and spied all of her again, she didn't think she could restrain herself.

Adia tipped up onto her side, her bosom pressing into Elise's shoulder.

"Is something wrong?"

A beautiful woman was in her bed. Nothing was wrong.

"No."

Adia's fingers traveled across her shoulder and down her arm.

"Watching that movie woke me up. Isn't that odd?"

"It woke me up too," Elise croaked.

Adia rolled back over to her side of the bed and let out a loud breath.

"What are we going to do to get sleepy? It sounds like we're going to have a busy day tomorrow."

Adia's playful words fanned the fire in Elise's core. She didn't need a second invitation.

"You've been through a lot," she said. "Tonight I will take care of you."

Adia smiled.

"You have already been taking care of me."

She wanted to taste the woman's essence, but entering Adia with her tongue might be too much for their first time. One hand fondled Adia's breast while the other sought her pussy. She sank one finger inside and swirled it around, feeling Adia's juices. The woman was attracted to her. She added a second finger and began thrusting slowly.

Adia spread her legs as wide as they could go on the bed without dangling over the edge.

"You're eager."

Adia sucked in a breath.

Elise didn't know whether to drag out their first intimate experience or send Adia plunging into ecstasy as fast as she could. She opted for the second choice. It would make her feel better to see the pleasure she brought to Adia.

She brushed her clit with a feather-like touch and Adia moaned. Elise's fingers twirled around the button. Adia panted, her bosom rising and falling rapidly. Elise marveled at the beauty that was coming undone at her touch.

"Yes." Adia moaned. "Yes. Oh yes!"

With all her fingers she played Adia's body. She rubbed and tweaked Adia's dusky nipples, dreaming about the day she could take one into her mouth. Adia's right nipple hardened and the left formed a peak as well.

Lower down. All her fingers probed Adia's mound, swirling and stroking.

Adia's moans grew louder and closer together. Elise knew her orgasm was coming. Adia screamed, the sound echoing off the thin walls. Heat rushed into Elise's cheeks as Adia's juices gushed into her hand. Her pussy clenched around Elise's fingers, and she watched as the woman she'd just met thrashed in the bed in mindless bliss.

When the aftershocks had ended, Elise withdrew her fingers and brought them to her lips.

"Sugary sweet."

Adia lay on the bed relaxed, beaming.

"I've never felt safe enough to let go like that. It was divine."

"You're staying here, Adia. I promise to give you pleasure like that every day."

The look Adia gave her in response said she was glad to consider more than a roommate relationship, at least for now. Together, they could take it slow and figure out their options.

Elise lay back on the bed and sighed happily. *So far so good*, she thought. She hadn't managed to take control just yet. Well, maybe a little. When Adia rolled over and snuggled into her side, Elise tugged her close in case the tears should fall again. Then she pressed a kiss to her forehead.

"Good night, Adia. Sweet dreams."

She dearly hoped the woman no longer had nightmares. The thought of saving her and women like her from horrible situations sent a rush of determination through her. Bringing Adia here was the right decision. She had to spread the word, organize fundraisers, and assist in relocating more women. From this day forward her business would do more to help women like Adia all over the world.

Shiloh Saddler is primarily a GLBT Erotic Romance author. She lives in the Pacific Northwest where she enjoys spending time outdoors. When she is on her laptop writing her cat acts as her supervisor. She believes love and a good book makes anything possible.

Cruising The Distance

By Evelyn Deshane

I tell people I moved to Waterloo for a lot of different reasons. When my Ph.D. proposal was accepted, their university offered me the most money. The apartment I found was comfortable and had a distant view of the sister city, Kitchener. The school met my requirements and would let me study pop culture from an academic perspective.

But it's all secondary to the real reason. When I was twenty, my ex-girlfriend took me to the art studio on campus and the art store around the corner. After, I shared a bed with her in a cramped basement surrounded by her paintings and her Women's Studies course readers. We weren't together. We never kissed. But I felt the electricity in the air, the spark of possibility.

All of Waterloo became that spark.

On my last day with her, she took me to one of her English Lit classes where they were studying the poetry of Dionne Brand. The professor looked at me as if I was an outsider, but soon shrugged and allowed me to stay. Halfway through the class, when the instructor explained that Brand loved women, a boy in the class did a head-cocking maneuver and raised his hand.

"But I don't understand. Can women be

homosexuals?"

Stacey looked at me and smirked. We held back our laughter in the class and only let it out once we had reached her basement apartment.

"Can you believe him?"

"I know, right? Oh, sweetheart," I said in a patronizing tone, "women can be homosexuals. Hah!"

Our eyes met again, but we still didn't kiss. Stacey became stiffly formal, as my time with her grew shorter and shorter. By the time we reached the Greyhound station, she had given me a brief robot-type hug, and a mumbled goodbye.

It's the distance, I told myself on the long bus ride home. *It's always the distance between us.*

I lived in Peterborough, a city three to four hours away by car, even longer by bus. I was attending a different university, with two more years to go. It was the distance.

I visited Stacey that weekend to explore Waterloo's graduate programs. On the bus, I took out the folded pamphlet and read over the options for graduate study. Inside the hallways of Waterloo University, I convinced myself we could prove everyone wrong. We could be together again like we had been when we were eighteen.

❧❧❧❧

I met Stacey online. I'd been posting on a music message board about a show I was going to be involved in—some Canadian knock off MTV reality show. I was going to be the main interview and human-interest story. It's embarrassing looking back. At eighteen I felt like a celebrity. I continuously posted about it online, but this message board was new. I was surprised when I received a reply about the show's repeat airdate.

"I saw that! I saw you," Stacey said. "Wow, this is incredible. How can you be so brave, and you live close to me!"

At the time, I was in Toronto and closer to Waterloo by public transit. Stacey was still seventeen, in her last year of high school and feeling trapped by her conservative parents. She had a car. And she used that car to go to Toronto every so often.

"Maybe we can meet up sometime. Go to a concert or something."

"Yeah," I said. "Maybe."

We started to talk a lot. I knew I was interested in women—but it had been something that the TV show producers censored out of my human-interest story. When I told Stacey, I expected to find some resistance to my presence in her life, especially from her parents. Meeting a stranger on the internet from a big city, and knowing that stranger is a lesbian, screamed a parental interference opportunity.

"Don't worry about my parents," Stacey said. "They saw your TV piece. I just won't tell them you're gay." Thus started an aura of secrecy around us.

My desire for her was the blooming of her desire for me—the start of her realizing feelings that would never actually come to manifest physically, all complicated by distance. We put off our first meeting until some of our favorite bands came to Toronto. By that time I was already living in my university dorm.

Going to school put another hour of travel between us. Stacey was still attending high school classes. The distance enabled us to feel desperate, to feel bound to one another, and soon it was spilling over in her emails.

"I'm in love with you. Like for real—as a woman. I think...I think I want to date you," She wrote.

"I love you too. And yes, like that. We can...we can date if you want." I replied

"Yes. Yes. Yes," we agreed.

Our relationship never felt fraught like the long distance relationships I'd seen on TV. The barrier for us was always temporary, always outside of ourselves, and always with a time limit. I'd been with females in the past. Before Stacey's email confession I'd been trying to court a woman down the hall. Stacey changed everything for me. We hadn't met face to face yet, but we had the future concert approaching. A band we liked came to the city, and we bought tickets online. Only two months away. I stopped courting the girl down the hall and devoted all my time to emailing Stacey—to waiting, to wanting.

A week before the show, Stacey sent an email with a blank subject heading—a bad sign from the start.

"I don't know if I can do this. I don't think I'm gay. I just don't...I don't love you like that."

I closed the email. Desire that had been kept alive by our sparse internet connection felt severed. She loved me, but she didn't want to fuck me. The frustration bloomed under my skin.

But I had the tickets. We had the music. So I went to the show by bus, and at the concert, we barely talked. There was always a wall between us.

❧ ❧ ❧ ❧

I used to think I could only cater to my desire online. I never went to gay clubs because I didn't drink and because most of my friends were straight men who never wanted to go to clubs. So after Stacey, I searched the internet for women. I wanted to fall in love. Not fuck—but fall in love. The dull ache of a broken heart turned into an angry free fall. My future with Stacey was over. I searched for a replicated feeling of love on Plenty of Fish, OK Cupid, and on the same music message boards where I'd found Stacey—or really, she'd found me.

Diana was next. She lived in Upstate New York and worked at a drug store during the night shift. I fell in love talking to her about her family, her quirky sister, and her growing up in the queer community. She was gay—out gay. She'd headed the LGBTQ group at her school, which organized secondary proms for queer kids who never got to go. She wasn't going to run away from her desire like Stacey.

And she didn't. She took a Greyhound bus to Toronto three months after we declared our mutual desire over a computer screen. I met her at the station. She greeted me with the hug I never got from Stacey. We took the train back to my place and spent a week in bed. After saying goodbye to her at a Greyhound station, the sudden plunging ache in my stomach took me by surprise. We'd been dating three months, and saw each other in person for one week. Love so soon?

I felt the gut punch as I said it, told her I loved her. And in the absence of a reply was her silence.

I took the train back home, the distance between us, seemingly never-ending.

We broke up a month later.

One day, another email floated into my inbox with Stacey's name on it. We made plans to meet up a week later—this time, as friends. She'd grown up a lot from the seventeen-year-old who hated her parents and wrote fan fiction in a notebook during high school classes. She was now an artist, and Women's Studies minor, and a Fine Arts major. She was utterly beautiful. Her mousy blonde hair had been dyed black and cut into a severe bob. She wore blood red lipstick and dark eyeliner. She'd started getting tattoos. She was a woman, now—not a young adolescent.

We met in downtown Toronto and got vegan food at a cafe. We went shopping. We caught up. And when I left to get on the train back home, she hugged me tightly. The distance between us evaporated, and the sucker punch to my gut got me again. I was still so in love with her. I was still attracted to her.

But she was not and never would be attracted to me. Not like that.

So we became friends and nothing more. We met up every few months and hugged and everything seemed fine. Every time we got too close, she'd pull back. Her hugs became like robot arms, and her words sparse in emails until eventually she'd send one with no subject. We'd be intense, and then she'd pull away. Six months later, intense again, and eventually she'd pull away. Somewhere in the middle of the coming and going of our relationship, we went to Waterloo together. I'd tried to plan for my future but couldn't resist her. Every new season, every new summer, I'd be on a train again to the heart of downtown Toronto my graduate school pamphlet forgotten and nothing but Stacey on my mind.

Then she got a boyfriend, a serious one. Once they moved in together, the emails stopped altogether.

It was after that I decided on the University of Waterloo for my Ph.D. I packed my stuff into a car my friend loaned me, and we drove to the city to set up my new apartment. I told everyone I was there for the money, the academics, even the largest lesbian pulp collection that the university had in its basement library—anything but the real reason. The real reason seemed stupid and hopeless at best, and creepy and overwhelming at worst. I was repeating the past hoping to get a different outcome. I was trying to relive something I'd never had.

I unpacked boxes of clothing, and found some of hers mixed with mine—and boxes of her letters and her art. She was always there. It wasn't long before I was googling her to find out if what I remembered about her life was still true. She was no longer an apprentice at the tattoo shop. I had no idea where to find her. She'd slipped away from my radar…from my life.

A sinking feeling hit my stomach a familiar sense of dread….a sensation like she was gone.

There's a hill leading up to a mountain, thirty minutes from Waterloo, where the city of Hamilton is visible from the climbing highway. A point where the world seems utterly open and ready for the taking before it all drops as the vehicle you're in moves on. The view is beautiful at night, completely lit up and shining on the mountain. I always longed to see the mountain each time I made the trip.

But as I moved to Waterloo and felt Hamilton drop underneath me, I realized I wasn't a passenger anymore. The movement was permanent, not enabling. I would be sharing the same space the same hometown as Stacey now. In the back of my mind, I'd tried to forget this. I tried to pretend that we were exes who never talked. I wanted to avoid her hangouts around town—the tattoo shop where she was supposed to work—the marketplace where she bought vegan cheese. I pretended I could shun the city's black holes that she frequented, walking around them like a ghost.

But I wanted to see everything in front of me and haunt it with hope.

Then lose it again…and again…and again.

My heart's desire could never be satisfied by another, it was always on buses, on trains, on public transit as I waited to see Stacey, the only person I wanted. As I waited, desire bloomed, and potential was everywhere. On the bus, I could imagine the perfect queer horizon—the thing Jose Munoz talks about in his work—and I could believe it was possible, for a moment, before it was out of reach.

My long distance love was really about distance, not love. Because even when we were in the same city, we didn't talk to each other. Even when the unthinkable happened—and I saw her from a city bus outside a store two years later—I didn't approach her. I looked at her dark hair, her many tattoos, and beautiful face. I didn't go over and ask her how she'd been because it was never the point. I wanted to be in Waterloo because of potential, not union.

We were always going to be in a long distance relationship, even in the same city, until I just let go.

❧ ❧ ❧ ❧

And letting go, as I've come to realize, is all about the stories we tell ourselves.

I wandered into the basement of the university's

library so I could view the archive of lesbian pulp novels. No matter how many covers I saw, I kept thinking of *The Price of Salt* by Patricia Highsmith and the man perpetually following them on the road, recording their private moments using it as bait. I wanted to be that visible—that noticed—and that accepted as someone who loved women.

But I never needed the third man, the third party recording the evidence like I thought I did.

In the book, Carol and Therese had fallen in love in Waterloo. It was the man tailing them, recording them, who tried to ruin everything they'd built.

I had always doubted my desire, trying to string it through a realm of experiences that was and yet wasn't my own. I wanted to be in love with Stacey because being in love with her was the closest I had felt to desire without being watched—being a lesbian without the male gaze entering into it, and rendering it a public spectacle. The private moments we shared never went anywhere because we were still too busy in public moments trying to show her asshole classmate that of course, women can be homosexual! Obviously. Just watch us.

It was always for public notice—but in reality, I never needed that. I'd been called gay from cars and lesbo since I was twelve and in gym class. I didn't need an identity label or even love. I needed desire outside of the heterosexual matrix. I needed cruising, but without the public transit.

About six months after I went to see the lesbian archive at Waterloo, I was waiting for a bus on the university campus. A woman with brown hair and a dark green jacket stepped close to me. Pretty, but most women I saw on campus were pretty to me. I saw the bisexual flag colors on a button over her jacket lapel—the feminist fist in her next button.

I imagined this to be a beacon announcing her desire.

I stepped closer to her. She noticed. Her eyes darted up and down my body. She cruised me with a hint of a smile. Desire.

Desire inside Waterloo, the city with potential—the city with distance—the city without a mountain, only the woman in front of me.

I smiled. We waited for the bus.

When the driver arrived, I followed her inside.

Evelyn Deshane has appeared in Plenitude Magazine, Briarpatch Magazine, and Bitch Magazine. Evelyn (pron. Eve-a-lyn) received an MA from Trent University and is currently completing a Ph.D. at Waterloo University. Follow @evelyndeshane or visit evedeshane.wordpress.com for more info.

The Letters

By Susan McLachlin

Later on, Livy acknowledged she wasn't ready for them when they finally arrived at the house. She knew they were coming. She'd been waiting for them for some time. That didn't make it any easier. She signed for the delivery and stood on the porch waiting for her anxiety to pass before she opened the box and gently retrieved the letters.

Shivering and cold from the bitter New Hampshire weather, Livy closed the front door behind her and held on tightly to the pile of letters tied up with rough twine. She stared at them and took in every detail, standing there avoiding the pain of reading them just yet. The letters worn around the edges were ink smudged from rough handling and torn where someone had inspected the contents. She turned the pile of them over and over in her hands. Forcing the courage she needed to move into the living room, she took them to her place by the fire where she found comfort. Livy stared out the window at the leaves that strained to stay on the branches in the September wind, and she remembered.

"Livy, would you please turn and look at me, I'm leaving? My driver is waiting, and we don't have time for this! Livy, please, I have to go!" Dancy paced back and forth in front of the door running her fingers through her auburn curls. Her pain radiated from her like the thunderous sound of a foghorn in a storm.

"No, no you don't," Livy said. With her usual quiet determination, her back stiff and unyielding. "We've been through this so many times that I have nothing more to say to you." She held her place. Her back arched in response to Dancy's leaving, her face remained calm refusing to acknowledge the confusion she felt inside.

"I can't go like this. Honey, it could be months, not weeks. Don't make me leave without holding you. You're making this so complicated when it doesn't have to be. Livy, please come to me."

Livy held her place in the impasse that they had created, and she was immobile in her anger, locked in her hurt.

Dancy carefully buttoned her long military coat, anticipating the cold of the rainy fall weather. She placed the last suitcase marked Doctors without Borders, Dr. Danica Ostrum near the front door.

In frustration, she quietly exclaimed, "I can't make this happen if you won't let me, Livia. I can't offer anything more than I already have."

Dancy stood behind her waiting for the unhealthy atmosphere to shift, for a reason to follow Livy's anger and her fears, but there was no mercy left here. Bereft and determined Dancy picked up the weighty medical case and headed to the door.

"Honey." She paused. "Honey, I love you, and I hate how this has turned out. I'll write, there is no cell coverage in that part of Nigeria.

Livy stopped in mid remembrance and thought it wasn't always like that. We came through the tough moments with gentleness, respect, and laughter. She paused while an old image of Danica laughing at their party at Monroe Beach came into focus.

Sun tanned and surrounded by friends, Dancy could make everyone feel welcome. She would provide laughter for the crowd, and crazy stories of her years of training to be a doctor. Livy, more the introvert of the two of them would often feel a bit lost among their boisterous crowd. Dancy would not let her sit in the shadows. At the party, when Livy hid in the kitchen tent, Dancy pulled her outside and initiated a slow dance without music.

"You could always bring me around in an instant with that beautiful crooked smile, couldn't you?" Livy mused, still cradling the letters, still not ready to open them.

They had met two years earlier through an online meet-up site that afforded LBTQ women of a certain age, with similar interests the possibility of finding romance, or at the very least a friend. Livy, who worked long hours as a surgical nurse specialist had no time for dating or relationships, but her friends talked her into giving the site a chance. Livy had not dated in over four years, relying on friendships, her volunteering or solitary activities like hiking to fill what little time she had after work. There was emptiness within her as the time passed without another woman in her life. No matter how active Livy's life could be, she missed the feeling of having a lover in her life. After unsuccessfully cruising the site for months she considered giving up on ever finding anyone there. Then Danica's profile appeared as she was preparing to dump the site altogether. It was hard for Livy to date someone who didn't understand the complexities of on call duty, yet the prospect of dating another medical professional like Danica gave Livy hope that perhaps this new woman might be more understanding of her commitments.

Carefully she read the profile. She checked out Danica's social and professional online presence and noted that they had a lot in common. Livy liked the casual, handsome look in Danica's profile pictures. She liked how she seemed to be serious, maybe even sorrowful. Then in another photo, Danica's smile belied something deeper, something worth exploring. Livy smiled to herself enjoying what she was seeing. She noted that Danica was tall, older than Livy and athletic looking. There was a hint of self-assurance that Livy found attractive. Dr. Danica Ostrum mentioned that she liked to dance. That she was not in a hurry to run headlong into romance or to ask for long-term tomorrows. Danica came from a large family, had political sensibilities similar to Livy's, lived in a city in Vermont and thankfully was not vegetarian. She listed her pet peeves as mindless conversations with dull people at conventions, a family that voted Republican and women who showed up on the second date accompanied by a U-Haul full of their belongings. With only minor misgivings, Livy wrote back to Danica.

Their correspondence continued sporadically for some months until a call came through while Livy was at work.

"Hi, may I speak to Livia Archers please?"

"Speaking, how may I help you?"

Livy said with irritation, not paying attention to the caller while she put away the files she had been sorting. It had been a long day, three surgeries and a run in with an administrator. She was not in a mood for more interference. Livy approached the crowded nurse's desk, in the same clothes she'd been wearing for fourteen hours.

"Hi. Is this a bad time to chat? I know you are at work. I won't keep you long. It's Danica. Danica Ostrum, calling. It sounds like I got you at the wrong moment." The noise in the background was deafening.

Livy was startled into paying attention. "No, no this is a good time. I need to get somewhere I can talk. I'm right in the middle of the mayhem here. Can you wait while I find a place and call you back?"

"Sure. On second thought no Livia. I'm in town, and I know it's short notice, but I wonder if you have time for a drink this evening, or perhaps dinner?"

"Hang on a sec." Livia moved into the supply room, closing the door. She breathed a sigh, thought for a heartbeat and continued talking.

"Danica, I'm sure you know what I mean when I say my scrubs reek, my back hurts, and I am no sight for sore eyes. I've been in surgery most of today. Maybe we should do this another time?" Livia laughed as she rubbed her eyes.

Laughing as well, Danica replied. "Yes, sure do understand. The thing is Livia, I'm only here until tomorrow afternoon. I've been delivering triplets on the west wing fourth floor of your hospital since early this morning. So I reek, my back hurts, and I am no sight for sore eyes. I want to meet you. Any chance at all? I want to drink, eat and sit across from you, fascinating woman who found me online. Your profile pic probably doesn't do you justice. I can't go home, not knowing if I'm right."

When nothing came from Livia but silence, Danica spoke. "You have to eat, right?"

"If I can stay awake, yes," said Livia.

"Then come eat with me. We'll make a pact to not judge the other on the degree of reek and tiredness. Whaddya say? Can you make that leap to a dinner out and perhaps the start of something special?"

"How can you be charming after a day like this?" Livia slid down to the floor, twirling her hair around her finger while she thought about her answer.

"Come have dinner, and you can grill me then. Right now I need to shower. Shall I pick you up or are you independent enough to meet me at the restaurant of your choice?" Danica said. The playful sarcasm was in her tone of voice.

"Oh you are good," Livia said, as she considered which restaurant would be the best for a first meeting.

"Okay, I get to shower and dress in something better than scrubs. You're not meeting me in scrubs are you?"

"No, I will do my best to make a decent impression," Danica said. "Where are we eating, and you haven't told me if I am picking you up?"

"Nice place on the waterfront, called Medicina. I'll meet you there when you text me the time. You can make the reservations. Oh, and I'll be the tired but good-looking woman walking through that front door. That work for you?" Livia was smiling as she waited for the response.

"Works perfectly," Danica replied. She was feeling very pleased with herself. "I'll see you there."

The fall day was drawing closer to the evening. The shadows lengthened across the Berber rug. Livy got up to turn on more lights and walk around her living room as she remembered more of that evening when they first met. She carried the letters with her, still not ready to open them. She stoked the fire and rested her forehead on the mantle.

Livy remembers that first dinner date as being both funny and chaotic. She had gone home, showered and dressed in the best dress she could find in a wardrobe not made for dating. Livy fussed over her weight, styled her straight blond hair then headed into a date that would ultimately change her life. She remembers being slightly anxious and curious about this woman who was so sure of herself waiting until the last minute to ask her out. All through the taxi ride to the restaurant, Livy questioned her decision to meet with Danica. By the time she walked through the front door of Medicina, she was wary and slightly irritated to meet this woman after a long, exhausting day. As she looked around and saw the face, she remembered from the profile photos, all the reticence quietly evaporated.

Standing in her living room, Livy softly smiles as she remembers the look on Danica's face when Danica watched her approach their table.

Danica had been reading the menu when she looked up to see Livy coming towards her. She leaned slightly forward delighted by the appearance of this woman. She was watching her as if she was the only beautiful woman in the room. Livy saw her image reflected in Danica's expression and took her time walking the distance toward her future lover. Walking with purpose and confidence prolonging her arrival she could see Danica's desire for her. As Livy walked the last few feet towards the table, no matter what the evening held, she had made the right decision. But as she was almost to the table Danica suddenly stood up and stepped out into the aisle to greet Livia. Her hand thrust forward to take Livia's hand. It was the exact moment that their waiter arrived at their table with a tray of glasses filled with water. The ensuing collision sent the tray forward into the aisle, the waiter careening into the next empty table, and water projected all down the front of Livy's dress.

Chaos reigned down, and the greeting turned into a scene from a Marx Brother's movie. Both women looked at each other, first in horror at what had just happened and then both burst into laughter at how ludicrous the whole situation appeared. The waiter flailed around trying to regain composure. Danica attempted to help him get back on his feet, and Livy hunted around for something to dry her wet clothes. Eventually, after Livy had returned from the restroom to attempt drying her dress, they settled in for an intimate evening of wine, food, and laughter. In the years that followed, they told friends this was the beginning of the exhilarating roller coaster ride that made their relationship and their marriage stunningly beautiful.

In her need for fortification, Livy opens a bottle of red wine in the kitchen and remembers Dancy's unusual grace at doing this task. She could see Dancy's strong, skilled hands manipulate the process like a well-choreographed dance routine. Then she drifts in her thoughts to those times when those hands caressed her bod. When being physical demanded everything they had to give to each other. They shared delicious wine, crisp sheets, long moist kisses and deep, unrelenting orgasms that stayed in Livy's memory long after Dancy had flown to Africa.

When did it all unravel? When did we face that fork in the road of all that shared happiness? Livy thought as she sipped the wine and remembered how it all started.

"You have got to be kidding!" Livy shouted, throwing up her hands in frustration.

"Hold on Livy. It's needed and you know I've wanted to help for some time now. The numbers Livy, the sheer numbers of horrific rape pregnancies and the lack of medical help, is catastrophic. I can't be who I am and ignore the call for help." Dancy explained this as she paced in front of Livia.

"Nigeria, Boko Haram. Are you out of your mind? Everything I've read, everything that comes up in the news says this is a slaughter ground for terrorism. What are you thinking?" Livia shouted into Dancy's face.

"I can't stand the thought of all those women without medical help, Livy. Someone has got to make it better than it is. Even by doing this, by going to help deliver these unwanted babies, to tamp down an already impossible situation, just maybe something decent might come out of this for these abused women. If I can go with the army and serve long enough to get them safely through another trauma, then I will come home feeling like...well feeling like we showed these women they were not forgotten by the world. I'm proud to be asked, Livy. I'll be okay. I'm not the only person going. I've got a military team behind me, protecting all of us." Dancy sat down next to Livia on their couch.

"You are insane, I swear. And selfish too! What if you are injured or...or...taken by them too? Or dear God, what if you get killed, Dancy. Had you even thought how I would deal with this? Have you considered for one moment how your family or I will cope? Dancy, you can't agree to this. It's just impossible!" Livy stammered and reached out to hold Dancy close. "Please, please don't consider this further."

Dancy held her partner close to her and tried to soften the conversation.

"Livy darling," she said, whispering in Livy's ear. "I have to go. I won't feel settled inside unless I do. Honey, I love you deeply, but this is what I trained to do, what I grew up wanting to do. My whole life has been about helping. I can't just stop being who I am. Honey, you know that."

Livy gently pushed her away, looking into her sad green eyes. "I won't agree to this. I just won't. You're not a spring chicken, my dear, and neither am I. I don't want to lose any time with you. Can't you understand that? We have this beautiful life, Dancy. We have rewarding jobs, this incredible home, good friends and family who love us both. You are supposed to retire dammit! Why do you want to mess that all up?"

"Livy, it's not a lifetime commitment. It's a short haul assignment. Most of the women were all impregnated about the same time. All the birthing will take place over a couple of months at the most." And in trying to change the conflict, Dancy smiled. "Besides I have excellent insurance, and you'll be a catch if I die."

"Danica, that is not funny! Don't even try to joke on this. I do not agree with it!" And in raging disappointment, Livy left the room. Danica shook her head, set her jaw in determination and made the call to Doctors without Borders.

Livia finished the glass of wine and carried the empty bottle and the glass, and the letters back to the living room. The streetlights had come on, and she closed the heavy curtains against the chill outside before she stoked the fire once more. Sitting down, watching the flames rise and fall, she considered.

Maybe I could have stopped her then. Maybe if I had held my temper, found another way to explain that losing her love would be the end of everything I hold dear. But she knew better because she knew her Dancy. She knew that once Dancy had succumbed to the lure of adventure paired with the possibility of doing great acts of humanitarian aid, nothing could have kept her here. Danica just had to be the hero of her tale.

It took three letters from Danica before Livy could swallow her pride and respond. The first letters from Danica were written apologies for leaving and stories of her work in Nigeria with the women who survived the Boko Haram kidnappers. Danica described the atrocities and the pain these traumatized women suffered. She talked about what it took to win the trust of women who endured constant rape and slavery before they returned home. Most were pregnant, and some were diseased and scarred for the rest of their lives. It was a constant battle to have the villagers accept these women and their babies, to see a future for the infants born from raped mothers. She wrote that the work was heartbreaking but so rewarding. She told Livy that she was completely sure that it was the right decision coming to Nigeria because Danica was receiving as much as she was giving. Her outlook on life was forever altered, because of this journey. And then she said. "Livy, the greatest thing I have learned here is that I am so blessed. I get up every day to a country torn apart by evil, and I wonder if I will ever feel clean again. The thing that keeps me stable, keeps me going is to know that I will come home to you. I have missed your morning chatter, your sweet touch on my skin and even your loud, wall shattering snoring. I know this has been difficult for you to understand, but Livy this country of extremes, this seat of the beginning of humanity, this extraordinarily beautiful continent. I would regret not having lived here, breathed the distinctive air and eaten such strange meals. When I come home to you, can we make all of this right? I'm bereaved. We are so far apart by even more than the distance. I love you so."

Livy wrote back "Stop fretting about us and do the job you were meant to do. I am sorrier than you could ever know that I let you go to Nigeria without my hugs and my good wishes. I cannot fully explain without crying just how your stories have shaken me to my deepest places, my love. Come home when your work is completed and know that I will greet you so much better than the way I let you go."

Their correspondence traveled back and forth for months. Their relationship gradually healed. Then in some strange way, it seemed to get less fragile and more intimate. Livy and Dancy became lovers in a whole different and exquisite way. The letters became a separate world for them. This brave new world of letter writing opened the hearts of the two mature women and offered them a freedom they had not fully understood until there was a great distance between them. The want and need for the other became more focused and full with an undeniable energy. Their commitment had a new depth and persistence. The homecoming would be spectacular.

Three months passed. The letters appeared like clockwork. Then they stopped. For some reason, Dancy wasn't answering Livy's letters. She suspected that the medical camp might have moved, as there was a terrorist activity to the north of its position. Dancy had written that Livy was not to be concerned, but the army was thinking of moving the camp farther away from any fighting. It would be a major undertaking, and none of the medical staff were looking forward to the difficulty of traveling with the pregnant women expecting birth at any moment. She cautioned Livy that the team might be unable to communicate for a while. But by the third week with no word from Danica, Livy contacted Doctors without Borders and asked for information on what was happening with Danica's team. They said there had been some complications with the move and they would get back to her when they knew more information. Livy patiently waited.

Two days later, Livy opened her door to find a representative from Doctors without Borders standing on her porch. Livy remembered the woman looked so serious that Livy found herself holding her breath and slowly reaching for the doorframe to steady her body. She invited the woman in.

"We know that Dr. Ostrum was in the middle of delivery when everyone else was ready to leave in the main convoy. She was determined to make sure that the very young mother would get care, so a couple of nurses and a small protection detail remained behind with her. They were all supposed to leave very soon after the main convoy. Unfortunately, there were complications with the birth. Dr. Ostrum radioed to the convoy that she couldn't leave the young mother. The woman had lost a lot of blood. Within the hour the terrorists overtook the camp. We lost contact with our people. Ms. Archers, I am sorry. I cannot tell you anymore at this time because we don't know more as of yet."

Livy searched the woman's face for reassurances that more information would be forth coming. She held her panic back. "How can you not know? What is being done to find out?"

"The Nigerian army is forcing the terrorists back. They should be at the camp by evening if everything goes as planned. But I am here to prepare you for the worst case scenario if the news is bad."

The woman stopped long enough to be sure that Livy had taken the news within and continued.

"There was shelling and a lot of smoke coming from the camp. We still have hope that they took Dr. Ostrum as a hostage. They do that when they know our organization or the government will pay a ransom for a doctor. I have faith that this is the case. You must not give up hope. I have seen this situation before. The Red Cross gets involved, and they look after our doctors. Let's hold onto all the hope we can muster for now. We should know more tomorrow."

The news was not good. The camp had been ransacked and burned. The mother, the baby, and all the protection detail left for dead. There was no sign of the medical staff. The word came they were being held for ransom, and the conditions for their release were unattainable. Things were under negotiation, and the Red Cross was there.

Weeks passed, and Livy continued to write to Danica. The terrorists didn't allow phone calls, but the Red Cross was able to get letters to the captives. Livy wrote every day with the hope that this would keep Dancy's spirits up and remind her that she was loved, and missed so very much. It was hard to know what to say, but she wrote.

"Dancy, we are trying very hard to move things along in the negotiation. There are many sticking points between our government and the terrorists. Everyone is making a huge effort in placating these people, but it's like falling down the rabbit hole in Wonderland. Hold on my love. We will get you all home as soon as we can. I have never been religious, as you know. I have taken to praying for a break through, praying that you have food and safety. I'm even trying to make deals with Heaven to bring you home. Yes, I knew that you'd laugh at that. Please hold on, Honey. I love you so. Livy."

The news came that the Federal government would not cede to the demands of terrorists. The negotiations ended abruptly, and everything went silent from all the parties concerned until the call came for Livia.

"The Nigerian army attempted a raid on a Boko Haram camp where the terrorists were holding the hostages. The mission executed with the full force of the troops was not well planned. It was a disaster. The terrorists slaughtered everyone they held captive. No one survived. We feel terrible bringing you this news. Dr. Ostrum and the rest of the medical team will all be brought back for burial. You have our heartfelt condolences. There will be a complete investigation. I know that will not be enough for you. I will have her belongings returned to you. It may take awhile. I am so sorry to be the bearer of this information and for your loss."

Livy went through grief as if she was weighed down with cannon balls. Her heart felt shattered. She knew she would recover, but it would take some time to get on with life. Eventually, Livy packed up all of

Danica's things, attended the ceremonies that honored the good work of Dancy's team and then returned to work. When the letters finally arrived, she was almost to the point of acceptance. She knew she would always be empty in the deepest parts of her heart.

The fire was down to embers when Livy finally opened the letters and began to read.

"My dearest Livy. I cannot tell you just how much your letters mean to me, my love. The days are endless and bitter here. We do what we can to help each other, but it's so difficult when they allow so little resources. We make do with what we have.

Livy, I don't know if this will turn out all right. We try to stay optimistic. It is tough to remain hopeful in these conditions. But you need to know that I will always be with you no matter what happens to me here. I have found a sort of grace in knowing that you are always with me in these letters from home. I cherish everything, every word you carefully compose for me. You are my shining light and my hope for our future. I promise you that I will wander no more (LOL) and that retirement means I remain on American soil with you, with my Livy, my best gal. I send you all the joy that I gather from your beautiful letters. I hope my writings give you peace of mind for as long as it takes to read them. So read them often my love, for I send the best parts of me home to you in these letters. Stay gentle and do not let this turn you bitter, Livy. We have so much living to do. I know you will embrace this beautiful life until I return. Love you so, my woman. Your Dancy."

Livy read the letters through the night. The fire died, but Livy remained locked into the words and sentences of caring that poured out of the letters. She felt again what it was to know her partner's strength and compassion in the face of such unbearable conditions. Livy wrapped herself in the sweetness of Danica's true nature and the comfort of her thoughts about their love. The letters would always be their bond. As Livy went forward into her future, she would carry no sorrow from the letters and remember the gift they represented. Danica would always be with her, always in the letters.

Susan McLachlin is a writer, a poet, and a theatre reviewer. She is semi-retired and looks fondly to the coming years of writing about senior LBTQ sexuality with total abandon. She lives in beautiful British Columbia and has survived two long distance relationships that brought her much joy.

The Train to Glasgow Central

By Kitty Kat

They say you never know the exact minute. When I stepped on the train at Largs station that day, I couldn't imagine that my life was about to change forever. Heading off for a day in Glasgow, I expected to get settled in a comfy seat, put in my earphones and wallow in a romantic audiobook. The journey usually took around an hour and the train would get progressively busier as we neared the city. I usually zoned out and avoided eye contact. I had been caught in conversations with strangers too often. What was it about me that encouraged strangers to tell me their life story?

As the train pulled away, I started my book and looked out of the window as the beautiful west coast came into view. I could see some snow on the top of Goat Fell on the Isle of Arran. At West Kilbride Station a small noisy group of people got on and found seats in the next carriage. A tall, attractive, dark haired woman traveling on her own ran onto the train at the last minute. Slightly out of breath she scanned my carriage for a seat and sat down opposite me. She smiled over at me and said "Hi, good morning. On your way to Glasgow?"

I must admit to being conflicted. I would have

preferred not to spend the journey in conversation. But the stranger had the cutest Canadian accent. Spending a lot of time in Canada over the years, my interest was piqued.

I couldn't believe how quickly the journey went by as we started a conversation that awakened something in me, something I had been fighting my whole life. She told me her name was Christine, and she lived in Markham, just north of Toronto. She was here visiting her grandmother and was on the way to the airport for her flight home. I told her about my trips to visit family in Canada and how I'd grown to love the friendly, welcoming people there. I showed her a photo of me doing the Edge Walk at the CN Tower and cycling around Toronto Island with my cousin Andrea. It was such an easy conversation. By the time we pulled into Glasgow Central Station, I knew more about her than anyone I ever met. I told her about myself, opening up to this complete stranger in a way I never had with anyone else. We said our goodbyes on the platform. I saw something in her eyes that stopped me from looking away. I didn't want the moment to end.

A heaving mass of humanity leaving the train meant we had to move. The moment was gone. My new acquaintance glanced up at the station clock, and a look of panic appeared on her face. She had to catch the airport bus just outside the station, and it was due to leave in three minutes.

"I have to go, or I'll miss my connection," she said.

"Yes of course. It's been lovely meeting you." I wanted to say so much more, but there was no time. What if I had misread her interest in me?

I watched as she rushed towards the exit, her long dark hair swaying. I felt bereft. There was something there, something between us, and I just let her walk away without telling her how I felt.

My day passed in a haze. I tried to get interested in shopping and lunch at a small Italian restaurant. I couldn't get her out of my mind. I felt as if I was on the verge of tears. What was I going to do? I'd always been attracted to women but had been too scared to act on it in the past. Maybe it took a bolt straight to my heart to make me see what I had to do. She'd still be on the plane over the Atlantic. She probably forgot about me already. For once in my life, I had to be brave and take the initiative. I was going to track her down even though we hadn't exchanged details. *How?* I thought.

Everybody is on some social media these days. That would be my starting point. I only had a first name Christine, the fact that she lived in Markham, Ontario and the image of her beautiful face burned into my soul. It couldn't be that difficult, eh? I fired up my laptop and went to work on searching the internet. On Facebook, I typed in her first name and her hometown but had to leave all of the other boxes blank. No results! What had we talked about on the train? Surely she said something that would let me narrow down the search? She came across as well educated, so I started putting in the universities in Toronto—no luck. I widened the search to all Ontario universities and still nothing. She said she had been visiting her grandmother who was Scottish. What if I started entering in Scottish surnames? Maybe I could find her that way. After typing in all the well-known Scottish names, I could think of—Campbell, Anderson, Hamilton, Ross, Fraser, McIntosh, Muir—I hit the jackpot. Sutherland.

Christine Sutherland of Markham, Ontario, with a degree in English Language and Literature.

After staring at her photo for what seemed like an eternity, I tried to find out what she said about herself, but there was very little information available. Her privacy settings blocked the details in her profile. I sent off a Friend Request and prepared to wait. After three cups of coffee, half a packet of digestive biscuits and what seemed like a mile paced back and forth on my living room carpet, my laptop pinged. Friend Request accepted. Now What?

She must have just landed at Pearson Airport and turned her phone back on. I took a deep breath and prepared to open my heart to someone I had spent less than an hour with on a train. I knew this encounter was going to change my life. I was scared. The overwhelming feeling of joy and completeness in my heart spurred me on. I opened up Messenger and started typing a private message.

"I can't believe I am doing this. I felt something between us today on the train to Glasgow Central. When I looked into your eyes, as you were about to leave, I saw something there. Please tell me I'm not wrong. There was a connection that I've never experienced with anyone, ever. I feel as if I've known you always and I want to know more."

I hit send and waited. I could see Christine typing a reply and grew increasingly anxious as I waited.

"You have no idea how overjoyed I am to hear from you, Fiona. I felt it too, and I can't get you out of my mind. I must admit I cried all the way to Canada and was so glad that the flight was half empty. I was able to get two seats to myself and make an attempt to hide my distressed state. I feel as if I can't go another day without seeing you. Is that mad?"

I could feel tears rolling down my cheeks and couldn't stop smiling. I met the woman I wanted to spend the rest of my life with, on what started out as just another ordinary day. The practicalities were for later. Now I was going to take a leap and find a way to be with the one person who made me feel complete.

"I want to be with you, Christine. I don't think I can wait." I texted.

"Then come to me. As soon as is humanly possible." She replied.

I logged onto the Canadian Affair website in hopes of getting a flight. Three days from now I could be with her again. I booked it quickly. Worried someone would beat me to the seat.

"I'll be there on Friday at 1 p.m." I typed.

As I emerged from baggage claim, I could see her. Her eyes were scanning travelers. My tears were already flowing. I could feel a wave of emotion overtake me. I was sobbing, and so was she. I held onto her and didn't want to let go. How was it possible to be utterly and madly in love with someone you barely knew? I was, and from this moment, nothing would keep Christine and me apart.

As we drove along the 401 towards Markham, we were both so deliriously happy. I couldn't stop looking at her, but my gaze kept falling to her lips. We arrived at her home, on a street of newer looking townhouses and got my luggage out of the car to take inside.

She barely shut the door when my hands were all over her. It was frantic and desperate. I was on fire. Our kisses were frenzied, and neither of us could wait. We discarded our clothes. An overwhelming need overtook me. I had to feel every inch of her, taste her.

As I looked up, her eyes burned with pure lust, but it was more than that.

It was more than just sex. For the first time in my life, I was making love, and it was the most amazing feeling. I will never get enough of her. She is everything.

Kitty Kat is a writer and poet living on the west coast of Scotland with her family. She enjoys walking in the hills and is an avid reader and reviewer. An interest in history and politics and a background working in Social Services influences her writing.

The Safe Girl

By Jennifer DeBonis

The year was 1996, and the internet was in its infancy. I was a line cook in a restaurant on a tight budget and computer illiterate. Despite this, I was intrigued by the internet with information at your fingertips and email. High costs kept this out of my reach. I heard about WebTV. A browser that connected to your TV and allowed you to surf the web and send emails. I was thrilled! It was as if it was made just for me. It wasn't cheap at over two hundred dollars, but it was much more affordable than a computer. At ten bucks a month for the service even I could swing that. I hatched a plot to have my parents buy me WebTV for Christmas. My mom was hesitant. This internet thing sounded like a den of iniquity to her. I staunchly maintained that it was the only thing I wanted and against her better judgment, she gave in. Thus began my transformation.

A little over a month later I was happily ensconced on the World Wide Web and having a blast. My favorite site was Six Degrees of Kevin Bacon where you entered the actor's name, and it tells you how many steps it took to get to Kevin Bacon. I also came across a book called *The Good Calorie Diet* by Philip Lipetz. It was based on the glycemic index and was simple to follow. Table sugar at a glycemic index of seventy was the baseline. Foods over seventy were considered bad, and foods below seventy were good. With ice cream falling under seventy, and a diet where there was no calorie counting, I was in heaven. Maybe I could finally master my battle with my weight. It's February 1997. I've discovered a whole new world on the Web, and I'm embarking on a new way of looking at food that doesn't require me to feel deprived. It can't get much more revolutionary than that, right?

I was expanding my horizons, taking better care of myself, and dropping weight. Even though life was looking up, I was still alone. It's February 13th and I'm home after a long day at work. I'm relaxing on my WebTV when I come across a dating site. My mind is blown to realize you can look at profiles and connect with people without leaving your house. Up to this point, my love life had consisted of a string of men I'd fallen madly in love with who either considered me a friend or didn't know I existed. I'd been in a lifelong battle with my weight and had never felt very attractive. All the men I found attractive were either taken or gay. I'd often say that I knew the type of woman I'd be attracted to if I were into women. I'd even said it out loud, to other people! At this turning point in my life, the day before Valentine's Day 1997, I thought *what the fuck, why wait any longer?* Onto the Women Seeking Women sections, I went. After looking at multiple sites without actually responding to anyone, I came across a lesbian message board. Right smack dab in the middle of the first page, I found her!

Her name was Liz. She was looking for someone to correspond with who was into the Arts and was intelligent. I was an ex-theatre geek and all my life I've been attracted to smart, artsy people. In our similar interests, our meeting seem fated. I composed a response, talking a little about myself and saying that I was reasonably inteligent, into theatre and films, and was a voracious reader. I took a deep breath, and I hit send. I never noticed that I misspelled the word intelligent. I'm eloquent, but not a good speller and in 1997 spell check wasn't prevalent. Luckily for me, Liz thought that was cute rather than stupid and wrote me back. There I was, flirting online with a girl!

Because this was the internet's early days, things were not very slick. This message board that changed my life was basic, so Liz suggested we switch to email communication. We carried out the first few weeks of our flirtation by email. The technology was so new that we had no way to exchange pictures. We became attracted to each other through our virtual correspondence, not because of looks. I was pretty worried about this as I still weighed more than I wanted to and was afraid I would disappoint her when we finally met in person. I committed to adhering to my diet. In describing myself, I mentioned that I was overweight but working out and losing weight and feeling good about my progress. Liz still wanted to correspond. I was giddy! Well more than giddy, I was falling in love.

Stretching my wings—check, losing weight—check, feeling happy—check. What could go wrong? As we became more familiar with each other, Liz let me know that her name wasn't Liz. Liz was her middle name, and Claire was her first name. She was using her middle name to maintain her privacy. Being an understanding Libra, this seemed like a reasonable precaution to me. I liked the name Claire much better than Liz and not just Claire, but Claire with an e, so much prettier than Clair without an e. Every day I rushed home from work in anticipation of a new email. We seemed to be on opposite schedules as it usually took eight to twelve hours to get a response from Claire. In a later email, Claire explained that although she was from Texas, she was currently living in Ireland. That was a bit of a bummer. I think Claire could sense that I was disappointed about the distance between us, though I didn't come right out and say it. Maybe things weren't so right after all.

I came home from work one afternoon shortly after this revelation and no new email from Claire. I was sad but thinking that if things cooled off, maybe it was for the best. She was in Ireland, and I was poor. How were we going to overcome that? Then the phone rang. I answered it and heard this lilting alto voice saying "Jen?" I knew it was Claire. That one simple word physically rocked me.

I slid down the wall to sit on the kitchen linoleum, both literally and figuratively floored by the sound of her voice. From that moment, I pushed all thoughts of giving up this connection, out of my mind. If I think about it now, almost twenty years later, I can still remember that feeling in the pit of my stomach—that fluttering, swooping, exciting, and terrifying feeling that hearing Claire for the first time engendered. Not with the staggering intensity that floored me, but with fondness and warmth, like looking back on your favorite Christmas.

That first call lasted about ten minutes. Claire was on a tight budget and couldn't afford to stay on the phone for too long. My budget was tight too, but talking to her was intoxicating so we spoke regularly and eventually I decided to pay for the calls. Along with the calls, we began exchanging letters and pictures. I took photos of myself to send to Ireland. She sent me a picture of herself. She looked like I imagined, tall, slender, and beautiful. She even had auburn hair and soulful, plaintive eyes. I've always had a penchant for red heads. Seeing her took away any doubts.

She seemed equally pleased with my looks and encouraged as many photos as I was willing to send. I was looking and feeling better than ever and became emboldened, sending a few semi racy photos, which were well received. I began to embrace the power of feeling confident, and I liked it. Claire and I settled into a routine of emailing daily, speaking every few days, and sending letters once a week or so. We talked about everything—politics, music, art, work, philosophy, spirituality, and hopes and dreams. We disagreed a fair amount, but the discussions provoked were fascinating. We were both comfortable enough in our views to agree to disagree. Claire was everything I was looking for in a partner. It seemed like we could overcome our long distance issue. She would be moving back to the States within a year and being on the same continent made anything seem possible.

It was time to bring up meeting in person. I had done a little research and visited a travel agent. I could scrape up enough money for a trip to Ireland. Breathlessly, one afternoon, I brought this up. Claire was very quiet. I immediately panicked, thinking I had ruined everything. I began backpedaling from my suggestion as quickly as I could. Trying for nonchalance, when inside my heart was breaking. Claire cut through my babbling to reassure me that she would love to meet me and that a trip to Ireland for that purpose was one of the most romantic things anyone had ever offered to do for her. One word from Claire, in that sultry voice, completely floored me, again. This time it elicited an anguished, heart-rending, sinking feeling, every bit as terrifying, but nowhere near as euphoric, as hearing her voice for the first time. Claire was in tears on the other end of the phone.

She said, "I've got to tell you something. I've been putting it off because I'm so afraid I'll lose you."

My frantic mind was throwing out all kinds of scenarios as I asked her what she had to tell me.

"I'm married," she said. That was not one of them. She continued to say that she was bisexual, as was her husband, John. They had an open marriage. She begged me to continue our relationship. She told me she loved me and pleaded with me to understand. Through my shock, I heard myself saying that I needed to think things through and that I would call her the next day.

I mentioned that I was a Libra. Perhaps I'd better explain what it means to be me. I'm the calmer of waters, the sorter out of problems, the seeker of all opinions, and the person who weighs all options. Should I have felt betrayed? Looking back, absolutely yes. In the heat and heartache of the moment, I couldn't bear to break things off with her. I decided to understand. I was seeing a woman for the first time, and she was a married woman. Something I would never have considered as an option before. It was her assurance that she and her husband John had an open marriage agreement that tipped the balance. It didn't hurt that she put John on the phone to tell me that himself. Holy Crap. I went from no love life to this predicament in the space of a few months. Life was indeed changing.

With everything out in the open, we agreed I would visit her in Ireland. She would take a week off of work and show me Dublin. She spoke with such passion about the city and the people. I was already transported there in my mind. We booked hotels and talked about the museums we would visit and the shows we would see. I put down a deposit on the trip. With each day bringing us closer to a physical meeting I was more in love than I'd ever been in my life. I was oddly calm about the sexual aspects of being in the same place with Claire, considering that she would be my first time with a woman. All I felt was anticipation, no anxiety at all.

Six weeks before the trip, Claire told me that John wanted to meet me. We had not intended to include him in any of our plans. Since I was going to whisk his beautiful wife off to spend many nights and probably a few days in bed with her, it didn't seem like a huge thing to ask. We could have dinner with the guy. After all, if I were going to be a lasting relationship in Claire's life, there would be details to work out. Transparency seemed the best way to handle things. Dinner, the night of my arrival was planned. Claire was over the moon, and John was pleased as well. Weren't we modern and open?

When the trip was a month away, Claire said that John had been pressuring her to ask me if he could watch us in bed together. I'm a very accommodating person, but this was going too far for me. I said no, flat out and Claire said not to worry. John figured I would respond that way, but thought he might as well ask. Misgivings began to creep in for the first time. Privately I thought that maybe this whole thing was just a little too crazy. Then Claire and I would talk about our trip, and everything else would melt away.

Two weeks before leaving, I had a sobbing Claire on the phone. John was feeling very insecure and threatened by me. He could see how much Claire cared about me and he was afraid that he would lose her to me. First off, total ego boost! Hooray me, for being that attractive and charismatic that he would see me as a threat. Then we started talking more about it. The whole sordid story finally came out. It turns out Claire and John's agreement was a little more limiting than initially expressed. Up until that point, it was a license to swap partners with other couples. It had worked well for them until John broke the rules and set up a swap without consulting Claire first. John just sprung it on Claire over dinner one night, with two people she had never met before. John wanted to sleep with the wife, not the husband, resulting in another broken rule. Claire's post that I read on the message board had been the agreed upon payback for John's multiple transgressions.

As I'm trying to process all of Claire's new information and justify to myself the reality of still having a raw, aching need to meet her, she tells me that I have to call off the trip. She said they didn't expect it to happen this way. She wasn't supposed to fall in love with me. I was Claire's dalliance so she could even the score with John in their extramarital affairs. John couldn't handle what was going on between Claire and I. As I was all set to meet the love of my life halfway across the world, she was telling me that I would have to stay at home. Despite the crushing disappointment, I understood! I did. It was scary for all of us. Claire was unwilling to risk her ten-year marriage to John on six months of emails, transatlantic calls, and airmailed photos. I was heartbroken, but deep down there was a little bit of me that was relieved. Maybe I wasn't as cool with the situation as I had convinced myself I was.

We didn't completely cut off contact, we still emailed, but it wasn't the same. I seriously considered still going on the trip. I had been looking forward to seeing Ireland. After careful consideration, I realized that I wouldn't be able to be in the same city with Claire and not see her. I didn't want to stalk her. After all, wasn't I the reasonable one in the mix? I lost a few hundred bucks of my deposit as I canceled the trip and went on with my life.

After Claire, I learned about The G Spot, a San Francisco lesbian pop up bar on Saturday nights and took a friend with me to check it out. I'd been in plenty of Gay bars, but this was my first real lesbian bar. It was amazing. Bolstered by tangible evidence of actual women I could meet in person, I went back to looking at dating sites, making sure I was only looking at local ads. Claire began to fade into the background, and my social life began to pick up locally. I had some regrets, but I was still glad that I had answered that message from Liz seeking an intelligent woman. I was far more confident than I would have been if my first foray had been with a local date. I felt desirable and knew what I was looking for in a partner. I was in a much better place.

With the passing of time, I realized that Claire was the perfect first girlfriend. It was a safe relationship. I could have my cake and eat it too. I got to be in a relationship without having to leave the comfort of my home or be at someone else's beck and call. My girlfriend was an amalgam of fact and fiction crafted by both Claire and me to be my dream woman.

I experienced profound love and gained confidence while losing weight more easily than ever before because all I thought about was Claire. Now I realize from the moment I learned Claire was in Ireland subconsciously I knew nothing would ever come of the relationship. That freed me up to fall completely head over heels with no real consequences.

Claire was what I needed at the time. I remain grateful to this day. I have two regrets though. I still haven't been to Ireland, and I can't remember her last name. I would love to try and find her on Facebook. It's probably for the best. I hope she is happy. I hope that she still thinks of me every once in a while and smiles.

Jennifer DeBonis resides in the San Francisco Bay area. She dabbles in writing in her spare time along with photography and hanging out with her dogs.

Distant Dreams

By BL Clark

The night is cold here, winter has set in, and the fire does little to warm me anymore. The only thing that warms me is the love of Kamryn Davis. She is my true love, my one and only. The challenge, my true love and I live half a world apart. I'm in the United States, and Kam is in Tasmania. I suppose that one of us could move to be with the other. At the moment this isn't possible. Kam's life and our relationship are complicated.

Kam and I have been together for almost a year and a half. We met online through a mutual friend. I was pining for someone who didn't want me the same way I wanted her. Her name is Carly.

"Lucy, it isn't that I don't care for you, we just aren't right for each other at this time. My life is about playing the field and seeing what new adventures are out there. Your life is more, um, stagnant."

"It doesn't have to be, Carly. Yes, I lead a tamer life, but part of that is you never want me involved with the things you're doing."

"It isn't that I don't want you there, it's that I don't think it's things you would enjoy," reasoned Carly Painter.

"Yeah, well, your point is clear." I relented.

Carly wasn't entirely wrong. My life was tame, compared to hers. I wasn't out there going to the clubs, going to the mall, going hiking, and all those things that outgoing people do. I was more into staying at home, reading, writing stories for fun, and playing online. I didn't have an aversion to going out in public. I just hated to be out there alone. I'm self-conscious and always worry that people are judging me. People may be too busy dealing with their own lives to judge me, but that's where my socially phobic mind goes.

I wasn't always this way, but if you got hurt and burned enough times you pull inside yourself. I was getting good at pulling away from the world before I met Kam. God, she changed my life. Kamryn Davis was a friend of a friend. We met when our mutual acquaintance was going through a rough time in her life. We were both helping and supporting her. I got concerned that Tasha, our mutual friend, was getting too depressed and sent a message to Kam. We started talking about ways to help Tasha, and it moved to us talking about our likes and interests. We had a lot in common.

Kam and I were both into computers, both into sports, and we both loved to write. Yes, the moment she told me she was a writer I was in heaven. I rarely met anyone who had the same love of books and writing as I did.

"You know, there is nothing better than the feel of a book in your hands and the smell of the printed words on a page," Kamryn stated, with conviction.

"I couldn't agree more," I said.

We talked for a long time over the span of several days just getting to know each other. As we talked, I learned that Kam separated from her wife and they shared a young daughter. Kam was committed to being there for her daughter no matter what. Her wife told her that if she were to bring anyone else into her daughter's life without her wife's prior approval, she would ensure Kam didn't see her daughter again. That threat would guide the relationship that Kam and I would build together.

"Hey, Beautiful," said the voice through the speakers.

"Hi, Baby," I said, smiling as Kam appeared on my desktop screen. Her short, brown hair and gray eyes melted my soul. "I missed you."

"I missed you, too. Sorry I couldn't call last night. Gabby was sick," Kam said.

Gabby was Kam's four-year-old daughter.

"Sorry to hear that, is she doing better today?" I said.

"Yeah, she is. Kids are resilient."

"Yeah, they bring the plague germs to their parents," I said, laughing.

It was two weeks ago that Gabby came home with a slight sniffle and within days Kam ended up with one of the worst colds she swears she ever had.

"Keep laughing. I still may die from that damn cold." Then Kam gave a slight cough showing that there was still something lingering.

"You aren't going to die from a cold, baby," I said.

"You don't know that." I could hear the pouting tone in Kam's voice. I couldn't help but smile when I saw it on her face.

Kam and I talk online daily via voice and video. We do whatever we can to keep in touch. From the time she gets up until the time she goes home from work at night, we are rarely out of touch. That makes for some long days for me with the international time difference. When you are in love, you do what you can to make it work. Some days are harder than others. In this relationship, the good days outweigh the bad.

"I do know that, my love. I haven't spent long enough being yours. We still have years to go," I said.

"I can't live without you, either, gorgeous. How has your day been?"

"Long," I said, before going into details about my workday.

We spent the next few hours discussing my day, how her morning was going, our plans for the rest of the day, and how much we loved and missed one another. You would think that it would get old, but it doesn't ever. Being half a world apart makes the romance difficult, but not impossible. It improves our communication, which is an area lacking for most of my past relationships.

"You are beautiful, Lucy," Kam said. "I can't wait to see you in person and make love to you."

"Someday, love. You promised," I said.

"I can't wait to meet you. I don't know when we can get together," Kam said.

"There is no pressure. I'm not going anywhere," I said.

"I know. I'm not going anywhere either. I feel like I'm keeping you from having a full life."

"I'm here by my choice, Kam. I know I could go out and find someone here, but you have my heart and soul, and nobody will ever change that. What happened this time to make you question things?"

Kam has a habit of overthinking things when left alone with her thoughts.

"Nothing," Kam said, averting her eyes from the screen.

"Liar, now let's talk," I said.

"Beth and I had another argument."

"About?"

"About Gabby, about the state of our separation, about you…" her voice trailed off, and again she was looking down at the ground.

"Look at me, please," I said, waiting for her to look up. "Tell me about it, we have no secrets and talk everything out. Remember?"

"Beth is afraid that Gabby is being affected by our lack of intimacy."

"How's that? You're separated. You sleep in separate rooms." I could feel the pit of my stomach knotting. "Hell, you would be divorced if she didn't use Gabby as leverage to keep you there."

"That's the issue. Beth doesn't want us in separate bedrooms…"

"She wants you back?" I interrupted.

"Yes, she says for Gabby's sake. She also suspects that there is something between you and me and that is what is holding me back."

"I see," anger filled my tone. It's hurtful. I have to push aside the pain and deal with the fact that I don't have a say in this part of our relationship. I always remind myself that I chose this. Kam would have to do what is best for her and Gabby.

"Babe, please don't get mad. I love you. I want to be with you," Kam said.

"But if she uses your daughter to manipulate the situation, you will cave." Yes, I was a realist in this area.

"I've never said that."

"Kam, I'm not stupid. I know that you can and

will do anything for your daughter. I have never asked for more, or for you to leave her for that reason."

"I know you haven't and I'm grateful for that. I never want to have to choose between you and my daughter."

"There is no choice in that. Your daughter takes priority."

"I hate that it has to be this way."

Kam's voice softened, and I could hear the pain in her tone. I hated that our relationship hurts both of us. I usually set myself up to be the one that gets hurt the worst.

"I do too, but Beth is calling the shots for now. Someday, maybe, we'll be calling the shots for our life together," I said.

"I hate asking you to wait," she said.

"I know. It isn't easy at times, but you are more than worth it."

"I'm not sure about that, but I'll take it," Kam said, winking and making my heart skip a beat.

"So, on a hopefully happier thought, what are you doing for your birthday next week?" I said.

"Going out to my favorite restaurant and then getting some key lime pie for dessert from the American restaurant I told you about."

"Key lime pie?" I said.

"Yes, it's my favorite now."

"So, do I get the blame for turning you on to that as well?" I asked, coyly.

"Oh, you turn me on to a lot of things and in a lot of ways." Kam's voice dropped off to a sexy whisper. "But yes, the pie is your fault."

While key lime pie is common in the States and one of my favorites, Kam had never heard of key lime pie before meeting me. She had to go to an American restaurant in Tasmania to try it. The owner told Kam this was one of their newest additions and they weren't sure if it was going to be well received. When it was, it became a regular part of their menu.

"I'll take the blame. I'll take almost anything you have to offer."

"Mmmm, I do have a few ideas," Kam said in her sultry voice.

"Promise?" I asked.

"Yes. So, what are you wearing? I can't see all of you."

"I'm wearing more than I'm certain you want me to be wearing," I said, laughing.

"We should do something about that…"

"You have work soon, my love," I said.

"Yes, but you're already done with work, so I can get you all hot and bothered and not have to worry."

"True, but that gets you worked up, and then you accuse me of trying to get you all hot and bothered before work or trying to get your pants off," I said.

"Well, you have to admit that you do both on a regular basis."

"I can't help that you can't resist me. I can't help that you and I have the same dreams at the same time, feel the same things. We are meant to be together. The Universe just likes to fuck with us."

"I know. It'll work out," Kam said. I could hear the defeat in her voice. The romantic mood was gone, and all that was left was the hole that fate consistently punched in our relationship.

Kam and I are meant to be together. I have no doubt, but destiny isn't ready to let us be together. With Beth putting a wrench in our plans, or my visa getting delayed or the timing hindered by other outside forces, something always got in the way of us getting together in person. Some would say that the Universe was trying to send us a message. I believe that we must overcome the challenges, and then we will have our reward. I know it may be a dream, but it is all that I have.

⚜⚜⚜⚜

Another year passed, and Kam and I had finally figured out a way to meet, in person. Kam had a business trip planned to New Zealand, alone for two weeks. I was going to fly down and spend a week with her. She would be working for part of it, but I would still get to meet the love of my life and spend time with her.

"So, you have your passport, visa, and all your paperwork together?" asked Kam.

"For the tenth time, yes, honey." Every time we talked she verified this bit of information.

"I just don't want anything to mess up meeting in person," she said.

"You know as well as I do, the Universe is going to try to mess it up, but this time we will be together."

"I can't believe in a week I'll be physically holding you in my arms," she said.

"I know. I would pinch myself to see if this is a dream or not, but if it is, I don't want to wake up.

The week flew by, and there I was on a transcontinental flight to Auckland, New Zealand to meet Kam. The plane thankfully wasn't crowded, and the seat next to me was empty. I always hate flying in standard planes where you are practically sitting on your neighbor's lap.

Lucy: Hey Babe, just a quick message on the plane's Wi-Fi to tell you that I can't wait to get there, just eighteen more hours to go.

Kam: I can't wait. I think that Beth suspects something is up for my trip. She keeps commenting that I'm a bit too excited to be leaving Gabby.

Lucy: That's low. She needs to stop using Gabby for everything.

Kam: I know, but she isn't going to mess this up for us.

Lucy: I hope not. I hope the Universe gives us these seven days together, even if that is all we get for the rest of our lives.

Kam: We'll get more. I feel it.

As the plane got closer to my destination, my anxiety started to ramp up. Something Kam said once jumped into my head and was now plaguing my insecurities. She said, *"Sometimes, people in real life are so different than they are online...different to the point that it changes things."* No, she wasn't talking about us, but in a way, she could be...or my insecurities thought that it was plausible.

"Folks, we're about thirty minutes from landing, please start putting all large electronics away," said a voice over the intercom system.

"Oh, tummy now is not the time to start knotting and flipping," I pleaded with my body.

Once we were on the ground and I was coming off the plane, I felt this paralyzing fear building as Kam's statement about people being different in person ran through my head again.

"Well, it is too late now, I'm here, and she is supposed to be waiting for me."

I went down the escalator toward where Kam and I agreed to meet. That's when I saw her, holding a sign that said, Lucy. Original I know. I told her if she used any nicknames I was going to walk right past her and keep going. She must have realized that I was serious. As I got closer to Kam, I could see her trembling. I felt my trembles and fought past them as I wrapped my arms around her holding her close.

"I can't believe you're here," Kam said. She seemed to be holding back tears.

"I'm still not certain that this isn't a dream," I said and then felt a pinch on my backside. "Ouch! What was that for?" I said.

"Proving this isn't a dream."

We pulled apart, and Kam picked up one of the two bags I had dropped on the ground and took my hand with her other as we walked out of the airport. She held my hand the entire way to the hotel and up to our room. Our room. It had a nice ring to it.

"What do you want to do first?" I asked.

"Hold you," replied Kam as she lay down on the bed and motioned for me to join her. Our bodies fit together perfectly. More proof that we were destined for one another. We lay there for a long time, just content to be close. Then I felt her lips on my neck. It was a searing hot sensation. My every emotion and my extreme desire to be with her came alive.

"Dear God," I whimpered before her lips met mine. The kiss started tentatively at first and then became more heated and dripping with wanton need and desire.

We made love for hours before we were both too exhausted to move. Then we lay in one another's embrace, basking in the glow of our love. We made love several more times that night and into the morning. Kam had meetings to attend, and while she was gone, I walked around the city.

Hey, beautiful," I said, walking into the hotel suite and then realizing that Kam was on the phone. I tried not to listen, but I overheard parts and realized she was on the phone with Gabby.

"I'll be home soon, honey. I know it feels like I'm gone forever, but I got you a present." I smiled listening to the love that she had for her daughter. Her face shined with love and affection for this little girl. I don't have kids, so I can only try to imagine how that feels. "I love you, too. I'll call you tomorrow."

"You are too cute," I whispered as she stuck her tongue out at me.

"What, Beth?" asked Kam, the tension evident in her tone? "No, I'm not just staying away because I don't want to be near you. I'm working. Yes, I have a job, remember? Well, it requires me to go away at times, this isn't new. Fine, I will be home at the end of the weekend. Goodbye."

I moved and put my arms around Kam and kissed the side of her head, just trying to show her some support and love.

"I take it she isn't a fan of you being away?"

"Nope, but she is trying to play it like I'm doing it to get back at her and hurt Gabby."

"That's not fair," I said.

"Beth is anything but fair. She just wants to rip my heart strings to get her way."

"Yeah, well her way is to get you back. I'm vehemently against that idea."

"As am I," Kam said as she leaned in and kissed me softly. "Did you have a good day?"

"Yep, I did some sightseeing and then came back to see the most beautiful sight in the world, you." I was feeling a bit mushy. She brings it out in me.

The rest of the week consisted of the same. Kam would go to work, and I would go out sightseeing, then we would meet back at the hotel where she would call Gabby, we'd cuddle and discuss our day, then go out for dinner, then back to the hotel to make love and enjoy each others company. It felt natural, organic between us. Yes, I know that it seems that way with all new couples, but we had been together for three years. I know. Meeting in person for the first time cemented the deal. We were already one in our hearts, long before I came to Auckland.

On the second to last day that I was to be in Auckland, I woke with a sick feeling in my stomach. I decided to spend the day in the hotel instead of antagonizing my stomach. Kam promised to hurry back after her meetings. As the day progressed, I continued to feel sick to my stomach. I decided to run next door to the little store and get a cola to try to calm my stomach. When I returned, much to my surprise, Kam was back, and she wasn't alone.

"You have no right checking up on me. We are separated and have been for years. You need to back off. I'd divorce you if it weren't for Gabby," Kam spat.

"Oh, you just claim to love her when it is convenient for you. I'm the one who's been there for Gabby while you abandon her for work or whatever you are calling this," said Beth, motioning to the room.

"Kam?" I said, startling them both.

"Lucy, how long have you been standing there?" asked Kam.

"Long enough," I said.

"So, this is the famous, Lucy?" Beth snarked. I couldn't help but dislike her even more in person.

"Beth, stop," Kam snapped. "Lucy, I know this is a shock, it was to me too. Can you give us time to discuss this in private?"

"Sure, I'll find some sightseeing to do." I felt like shit, I just walked into my room and found my girlfriend and her ex, arguing and now they want me to leave. I saw the pleading look in Kam's eyes and relented. Without another word, I turned and walked out of the room.

I wasn't sure what to do with myself, so I went for a walk in the park next to the hotel. It was beautiful, but I couldn't appreciate it. My mind was back in that room wondering what the hell was going on. How had Beth gotten here? Why was she here? What was going to happen now? I still had a couple of days left on my trip.

Minutes passed to an hour, then two hours, at the three-hour mark I was done waiting and made my way back up to the room. It was quiet, eerily quiet. I opened the door and noticed nobody was in there. Had Kam come to find me? Had we missed one another? Why hadn't she messaged or called me? I looked around the room and found only my stuff. All of Kam's stuff was gone. There was a note on the bed. I picked it up. It read, "I'm sorry."

I stood there staring at the note for a long time, then my legs gave way, and I collapsed onto the bed. What was I going to do? Had she just up and left me here? How do you do that to someone you love? Should I try to call her? Should I wait for her to contact me? What the hell was I supposed to do? I had no answers.

In the end, I tried to call and message Kam but

received no reply. I finished my two days and went home, broken hearted. I couldn't believe she just left. I thought I meant more to her or meant something to her. I guess I was a fool.

It was a couple of weeks later that Kam messaged me asking how much I hated her. I thought about not responding, but I was still in love with her. I didn't trust her. I told her as much. She apologized and said that Beth left her no options. I told her I deserved better and she owed me more than two little fucking words. She agreed and said Beth had drawn up papers that would bar her from seeing Gabby. I didn't ask for details on how that would be enforceable. I knew when it came to Gabby, Kam would give in to Beth's demands. I didn't understand why she couldn't have told me this in the note. It would have made my life easier. I am still trying to figure out how one gets over the love of their life. I think I have finally realized that you can't, you can only hope that someday, some way, the Universe will see fit for your paths to cross again and for your love to flourish. So, now I embrace my love for Kam and pray to every god and goddess, that there is hope before we're too old to enjoy each other.

BL Clark lives in Southern Wisconsin. As a child, BL dreamed of becoming an author. She is now living her dream. In her free time, you can find BL working on various story ideas, or playing with some form of technology.

Website: http://blc.bkclark.net

The Lookout

By Dolores Maggiore

I chose to ignore the stink bug zigzagging its way through my field of vision framed by the floor-to-ceiling window. It had almost disrupted my fixation on the speck punctuating the flank of Mt. Hood's West face. Was she dead or alive?

The rescue operation had been going on since before dawn. It was impossible to focus my Swarovskis any sharper. I received strict instructions from friends and rescue personnel, to not go to the mountain. The haze was physical and psychic.

Individual ants moved. Colonies filed on their way. The Crag Rats Rescue Team and Hood River Sheriffs, I imagined. It's hard to tell which helicopters were which from my tower-like house sitting in the flight path for the nearby hospitals on Portland's Terwilliger Boulevard.

The whiteout locked me out of the immediate physical environment into the landscape of my mind. I shivered and moved closer to the gas fireplace. Its fan bleated out a mechanical vibration and percussion, creating an even greater vacuum. The isolation in my head was complete.

I shivered again, lost in the past, in a scene in Chamonix, France. We were not climbing on our own. I was never the climber. She was. Our guide was the Téléphérique Gondola mounting towards the Aiguille du Midi. Cordelia smiled at me making smudgy faces on the gondola's glass, kissing lips fogging the panes.

We drank red wine in the summit Café 3842, the wood and stone pinnacle refuge. We were perched, squeezed into and around the corner table. Our backs plastered against the thick windowpanes that magnified the peaks beyond. Had the glass given way we would have been human avalanches from 12,600 feet.

We had gone back and forth, tacking between shores. The slow dating method. Could I find work in Switzerland or France? Could you breathe in the States?

New York was one thing. No one and everyone managed to carve out impersonal space there, in a haze of seeming privacy. Oregon? I was in Oregon now.

Too close for you—too intimate, the very vastness of the waters and forests and glaciers fused us together. You could never stay there.

I would live in Annecy, France. Small and quaint enough for me, close enough but not too for you. You would still be able to breathe.

"Et le travail, ma petite Chérie?" You asked.

Work? Money? Words always fogged out the dream. No matter what languages I spoke. I couldn't find a job in Europe.

"Et l'amour?" I dared to ask since love was not a

word we bartered with often.

"L'air, la montagne, le ciel." You smiled, your eyes scanning the sky and Mont Blanc.

"Oui, ma chère. Of course, we'll live off the air and the mountain, and the sky."

"Pourquoi pas?" You joked.

And we did for a while—on vacations or if I had a windfall or you a sudden whim to cross over, to try a new way.

And then too many words, too little, or too much space. The closer we came, the less you could live. I desired that oneness with you. You wished to be one with the mountain.

❧ ❧ ❧ ❧

Once more together, present. We spoke little, neither in French nor English. We toasted again.

"Je veux rester ici, expirer enfin." You said you could stay and expire here, never in the States.

I heard instead "respirer" in French and agreed there was room to breathe here, albeit in shallow puffs. "Oui, en petites bouffées."

Our words were fleeting, our glances wispy caresses. To stay at the moment, that was life. Slowly evanescing.

"Tu peux descendre seule aujourd'hui. Pour une fois?"

I studied the reflection of the mountain in your sunglasses. I raised them to read your gaze. Your face softened with the warmth of the red wine. Did I trust you, asking me to go down by myself that once?

I shook my head. Our relationship had gone on like this for years now. You had endured the confines of your life beyond the lifts and gondolas, and summits of which you said you couldn't get enough. *Was it too long? Were the limits too narrow?*

I could not leave, not alone. You smiled reassurance and held my hand in yours, warmer, larger than mine. Your eyes were liquid lagoons. You said you would become the mountain one day.

You pointed to the chiseled peaks and pinched your fingers together.

"Solide," but melting. "Vapeurs" in space, open. "Libre," free.

I could never leave, not really. On the nights before departure I always stayed fixed in my spot on the brown suede butterfly chair, my eyes glued to the alpine glow on Mont Blanc. My words were a repetition, an echo of years gone by and going forward, "Pourquoi? Why?"

"Je suis avec toi. Tu le sais." You wore a soft smile, reassuring me that you were with me—in spirit.

"Oui." I swam in your eyes and stayed there. I never did leave—in spirit.

I carried you with me as if you were real. I lived in your space as if that was possible over three thousand miles away. I saw through your eyes and drank the wines on your tongue. I lost myself in you.

You were not there.

❧ ❧ ❧ ❧

Nearby skiers celebrating on hot wine let up a roar. Glass shattered. A window somewhere gave forth and crashed. Crystalline shards scattered. I lunged for your head, your neck.

Was it our window? What had you done?

A bead of blood swelled on your throat. It was not our window, our back support. It was not our time. A mere sliver of glass it was. Life went on with cheers of "Bravo" and "Zum Wohl."

I kissed you, your cut and your hands. "I have you. Don't leave," I sighed.

You smiled again. "Not today."

I put off the inevitable. I agreed to descend by myself, but first I had to hear the explanation of the crash.

"Toujours," said the waitress. "Triple glass inside gets broke. Pas de problème! They drink and smash! What to do? Eh?"

I bundled, zipped up the down-filled jacket—even in August—and mouthed the stem of my sunglasses to hide the beseeching glance your way.

You leaned in close to thread the scarf you had knitted around my neck and kissed me gently on my glossed lips. Caressing my back as you pushed me up from the leatherette bench, you whispered, "A tout de suite. See you right away!"

I knew that right away meant at least an hour, maybe more if the gondolas and lifts had long lines. Ice sometimes formed on the cables. There was that snapped cable in '78 or was it later? Some folks spent the night in an ice cave.

I never did well with separations. Never. I tried to relax into the sway of the gondola and the blur of the condensation on the glass. Scenes of years past and maybe years forward played out on the foggy screen in my mind.

Had we camped here only last year? Or was that five years ago when it had just begun? When did we travel to Spain to see the caves at Altamira? Was that after we painted my apartment in Paris?

And the plan we had to hike Mt. Hood and St. Helens? Would you come this time as you said you would? Is that for this fall or the following? Why did I get the feeling time was running out?

❧ ❧ ❧

Being afloat always did jangle my nerves. Still does. Maybe this house up here in the hills overlooking the Willamette and Mt. Hood was a bad idea. But I am warm and safe, and the anti-earthquake girders afford protection from shakes.

I laugh. The anxiety of those swaying gondola trips in France and memories of Cordelia transported me right back to Mt. Hood. To the drama of the moment unfolding here on the mountain in front of me, yet some hundred miles away.

Perhaps I would never know if someone had expired up there today. Or if the rescue teams had brought the person down—down, apart from the solidity and freedom, the oneness and the vastness.

❧ ❧ ❧

They never found your body. Not that day. You were still alive.

You did return to the car as you said you would. What a silly I was, you said, not to worry! We drove back in a hushed silence to Geneva, where we made love gently in the shadow crimson haze of Mont Blanc.

Your eyes twinkled in the morning. You reached over to your bookshelf to pull out the worn copy of Le Pettit Prince I had given to you years before and placed it in my hand. We held hands like that, still lying in bed.

"Remember," you whispered in English, "to look at the stars." You pointed out the window, squinting as if to see a star in broad daylight. "I am in the stars, all the stars, laughing and smiling at you."

≈≈≈≈

As I prepared to board my flight back to the States, Cordelia placed a gold star in my palm and winked. And now, the mountain, the sky, and the air twinkle with laughing stars.

Dolores Maggiore is the author of Death and Love at the Old Summer Camp, her debut novel, published by Sapphire Books, Spring 2017. She lives in Portland, OR and Borrego Springs, CA with her wife, Terrie, and Murphy, the rescue poodle, and Xander, the lynx point critic.

A Canadian Colorado Courtship

By Shawn Marie Bryan

The thrift store was alive with the sounds of a shift change. The volunteer staff was devoted to sharing the gossip of the day and the uncompleted tasks with their counterparts taking their posts. It was a relief to browse without one of the volunteers following me or offering help. Having their attention diverted allowed me to browse in a part of the store I had not wandered on previous visits. There were two garment racks pushed up against a corner cabinet. One contained awkward golf clothes, including hats and cleats on hangers. The other displayed almost couture vintage jackets, strange, beautiful, and tiny. The corner cabinet appeared clueless for a theme, with a few pocket games scattered around some office supplies. Then I spotted it. On the next shelf, pushed so far back it was almost out of sight, was a camera. It was a lovely fully functioning 35mm camera with a bag, strap, and four extra lenses. The sight of this sent me back to a place when a similar camera was both the answer and the end.

I hadn't expected to be courted by her. I didn't even think the conversation would go beyond the hour-long book discussion. Hosting a radio show with a book discussion format can get tricky when recruiting talk show guests. Some authors seem totally on board while others are a challenge. It can be difficult to shift an author from talking about themselves or their process to a discussion about their book or book topic. With my producer hat firmly in place, I seek out candidates that are interested or passionate about the book slated for discussion. These guests range from friends, colleagues, topic experts, to performers, musicians, and authors. The commonality, they are all readers. Even within the vast diversity of discussion partners, the official conversation is the one centered on the book specific to the show, routinely ending just in time for the outro and last sponsored spot.

In truth, continuing the conversation beyond the parameters of the show's format was rare. I can only recall four times the conversation legitimately continued. The first was with my good friend Jody Reale, with whom I co-founded an e-zine called *Saucy Chicks*. Since our conversation started long before the show and hadn't ever ended, it feels natural that we are still in it today and every day. Next, I gained two friendships with Authors Mary Griggs and Kieran York that began with phone conversations to discuss their books on the air. Finally, I was delighted when fellow radio host and mutual stats lover DeeJae Cox agreed to chat with me on a different show. Our passionate political minds didn't want to stop sharing. When this particular conversation turned into a courtship, I was the last one to see it coming.

When one of my most beloved books came up for discussion, I set out to find a stellar interview partner. It wasn't an easy task. This book adapted into a popular play and a critically acclaimed film had separate fan bases. Finding someone to discuss the original epistolary book without being unduly influenced by the play or the movie, proved difficult. I resolved to look through the members of a Facebook group devoted to the author. I requested the friendship of one member who I noticed spoke singularly about the book. After some time had passed and we started interacting on social media around other shared interests, I sent her a message about my initial intention for friending her and explained further about the show. To my delight, she was interested in the show and game to give it a try.

Over the next few weeks leading up to the show's discussion, we corresponded through email about the logistics, which exposed the need for slightly more in-depth communication. My new friend and willing potential guest lived in Canada, while I was in Colorado. Technically, this wasn't a problem as the station could connect us via a phone line. We wanted to make sure the international connection would be smooth. We thought about setting a test call, but the planning opened up several new topics to discuss, and we never did. We kept our electronic communication friendly and rarely about the upcoming professional engagement. Therefore our first phone call was the live one for the show. Looking back, I can admit it was during these conversations that attraction sparked and kept building. Even my buddy Kimmie mentioned I should be open to dating this person. I shot that down before she finished the sentence. We were merely researching for the show. I was a professional, and I thought she must surely have a partner. And she lived in Canada!

As far as shows go, the one featuring the dialogue between us was a pretty good one. We got to discuss a book we both truly loved and one that meant a tremendous amount to each of us individually. It was easy in that our banter and conversation flowed easily. I remember I didn't have to pull out any of my hosting tricks to keep the discussion going. My guest commented how fast the time went. It was fortunate that the show after mine was running a taped episode because we talked as if the time clock for the radio show hadn't been in play. When I noticed the clock and mentioned the time, she asked if we could chat later that night.

We did chat. It was as if our earlier discussion had smoothly continued. The conversation explored topics that stemmed from the book and delved into the personal. She had severed a relationship months earlier in a very definitive way. She said that once she made her decisions, she didn't go back. She said this latest breakup was final and she would not ever reunite with her ex. My heart, having gone down its bumpy road trying to remain firm in not seeing my ex, swooned at her decisiveness.

I kept myself at a distance. I wanted to be a good friend. Our communication continued as we talked about healing time, and freedom signs, and coming into more of oneself. It felt natural, like speaking with a friend I'd known for decades. We were eloquent, so much so that I almost saved the chat log for prosperity, or to make a little book of it for our friendship anniversary. That's a platonic reaction, right? What happened next should not have surprised me, but it did.

"You are such a surprise," she wrote. "What do you say to all of this?"

"To all of what?" I asked.

"You. Us. All of this," she replied.

I stared at the screen, not certain what she was getting at or perhaps not wanting to be let down by the hope that was bubbling inside of me. I typed a few starts of sentences and erased them. I didn't know how to respond. I purposefully didn't flirt with her, didn't want to cross the friendship line. She had been complimentary but nothing overt or lascivious. I barely allowed myself to admit it would be nice to meet someone like her and possibly date someone like her.

"Are you still there?"

"Yes," I finally typed.

"Then let me be very clear. Shawn Marie Bryan, I would like to court you."

Court me? Had we traveled back to an earlier time I had only read about? Did people talk like this now? More importantly, did a woman I was secretly exploring a growing attraction to say that to me?

"Court me? But, I thought we were just..." I tried to buy some time.

"No, you didn't. You feel this too. I know you do."

She was right. I did feel it. I did know it. My friend Kimmie knew it. Perhaps even the listeners of the show knew it. What I also knew was that my first girlfriend and I endured years in an excruciatingly painful long distance relationship. And my recent ex and I, with whom I'd had a commitment ceremony, had met through an online source. I'd sworn off both long distance and online relationships. Forever. I was trying to remain strong and committed to those convictions.

"I know this isn't ideal, us living so far apart," she said.

My thoughts spun, and I tried to deflect, even inside my mind. *Far apart,* I thought. She wasn't in the next town, or state, or region. She lived in a different country.

"I don't want to miss this chance. I would like to

see where it could go."

How many times had I shared with friends I wanted someone who was up front and honest about their interest in me? How many times had I longed for a glimpse of chivalry, something tangible, something lovely, something romantic, something true and something pure to build on?

My eyes blinked, and my breathing deepened. It felt exhilarating and risky. I promised myself I would never be involved in a long distance romance again. I had to admit it was exciting. My decisiveness to avoid online and long distance relationships, suddenly felt like an obstacle. I not only enjoyed reading what she desired, but I wanted to try it with her. I found the arrogance of her declarations decidedly sexy. Despite my many promises to steer clear, I let out a breath and typed.

"How does one agree to be courted?"

And we began, chatting online every day and speaking on the phone on specific dates. For weeks it was breezy and lovely. More than once I was reminded of the quote, "If you want to know a woman, read a letter from her." We were learning so much more about each other through this courtship. We led different lives and came from vastly different backgrounds and perspectives. That was exciting. I loved trying to understand her perspective on everything, and sharing all of my far-reaching pictures of the world.

"I am crazy about you," she would say or type to me at the end of every exchange. Its sweetness vibrated between us and enveloped me in a way that hinted at the beginnings of feeling safe. And though that doesn't sound super hot, it was included in the whole package, and that was plenty make-me-weak-in-the-knees sexy. For all of the things that were different about our lives and us, what we had in common was just as important as breathing. We shared our passion for the literary arts, our journey to discover the beauty of truth, and we were both on precipices of new creativity within our career paths.

We were both employed with enough resources to take care of our own needs. We shared the dream of finding new ways to add fulfillment to our lives. I started to envision an accessible, multi purpose literary radio station. She was beginning to embrace and expand her love of writing and photography. We were there for each other as we dreamed and planned and zeroed in on what we would need to fulfill these individual aspirations. There was something about being in a relationship that created a built-in space to dream about loftier goals while still going to work in our day jobs. There was something that made our relationship feel real and tangible. Alongside our dreams, we shared the mundane things in our lives, our annoyances, pet peeves, and practical needs.

So much of something that we snail-mailed notes and cards that further encouraged our feelings for each other. So much of something that we had discussed where we would live if this kept working out. So much of something that I had borrowed two different French language courses that I listened to studiously during my long commutes to the station. So much of something, we started to plan a trip to meet in person. I applied for a passport. While I waited for the passport to arrive, I had an opportunity to obtain a special gift for her, a tool for her trade—a tool she claimed in every conversation was the only thing holding her back from achieving one of her dreams.

Sending a package to Canada takes time and

costs a bit of money. I would gather little things and combine them in one box. One day, I started organizing a box of items with a DVD we both loved, a few literary tchotchkes, some postcards, and a silly ashtray we had joked over. With space in the box, I added the gift I had acquired for her trade. It was a camera, a good one, rather expensive though I had purchased it at a reasonable price. I was excited for her to receive it and start to use it to explore her passion. When I care for someone, my natural inclination to be a supportive cheerleader becomes heightened. My feelings for her were growing. I eschewed the warning in my brain, and from Kimmie that it was too extravagant too soon. I would do this for anyone, and especially for the person, I was dating. Feeling confident I sent off the package knowing it would take a few weeks to get to her.

"I wish you were just down the street, or across town, so I could get there in minutes to kiss you." We continued. Life continued. Our support and adoration of each other continued, as did our dreams and goals. We still had our phone dates, and we shared our relationship with other friends and family. They were supportive and happy it was working for us.

One day she said, "You don't agree?"

It was a simple question about something inconsequential. I can't remember the question, only that I did not agree. That started a whole new level of discussion in our relationship, one that prompted many long and dramatic conversations about what this difference between us could mean—did mean—and the consequences of it. We no longer talked about our dreams, their progress, and what we needed to achieve. We no longer shared how exciting it was to speak to each other about anything. We no longer ended every communication with her telling me how crazy she was about me, and my smiling within the feeling of being secure. Things had changed.

Then my package arrived.

In our phone conversation, she chuckled and was delighted with the objects in the package, including the camera. Then she casually said that the same day, a letter had arrived from her ex, asking for her back. The ex she swore she would never take back. Suddenly she said something that didn't sound right. Something was off with us. She explained that she owed it to herself and her ex to give it another try. She said even though her ex still wasn't entirely free, she was the love of her life, her true girl. She explained our courting relationship was no longer agreeing with her, that it was clear to her now that we could only be friends. And the camera, though loved and needed, was too much, too strange, too symbolic of what we suddenly weren't.

I could delve into some of the awkward ugliness that happened. I could share some bitter resentment. In the end, it was us acting out our negative feelings, those that we didn't know how to express. That's how I view it. If I look into myself with complete honesty, no resentment exists. Yes, this is the power of hindsight, and hindsight comes with the benefit of time and healing. It also comes with the beauty of acknowledging how valid, meaningful, and pure our long distance relationship was for each of us. I can only speak for myself, but I think she can sense this too, this palpable feeling that we needed each other for that finite moment and we are better people for allowing ourselves to go there, together.

Giving myself the freedom to explore a relationship outside of the expected tick-boxes helped me heal wounds I'd forgotten I had. I learned about balance and boundaries. I am no expert, but I established a foundation to build on. I wouldn't have seen the need for it had I not experienced this relationship. Both of us are still in our own countries, still pursuing our visions, still in our relationships with ourselves, as well as with others, and oddly enough—after plenty of space to heal and regroup—still in each other's lives. If I had not had those feelings for her—for us—at a distance, I would not have been able to recognize them up close when I was truly ready. I will remain forever grateful for our relationship as well as online connections and long distance relationships.

As for that camera in the thrift store that triggered these memories—I am tempted to go back to the store and buy it. I would use it exclusively to take pictures to help others see how to find the strength to get beyond the obstacles we set for ourselves—turn the photos into postcards and mail them far and wide. As for the camera, I sent to her—I believe she still uses it. She is talented and strives for an interesting composition and to capture the essence of the subject. She has a good eye…she spotted me after all! And together we both managed to create a snapshot that helped us fill out the bigger picture of our lives.

Shawn Marie Bryan hosts Women A'Loud! & Be(h)n's Book. She works in all media aspects: audio, video editing, production, narration. She's a Playwright, general manager for Network Listen, founder of twentyfourwords.com and a partner with Recognized Publishing. Shawn Marie and her love, despite being redheads, live in the California desert.
www.shawnmariebryan.com

Across the World

By Emerald

Simone found her addiction on lesbian dating sites. Over the past few years, this consumed her mind, her heart, and her pocketbook as she waited for the right woman to come along. In truth, Simone was quite lonely. For months she wrote poetry to women all over the world. Her craft was the art of seduction through writing. Alone in her cottage, she felt pangs of desire that wove a darkened web around her entire being, a pull towards something beautiful beyond sex.

Her favorite moments are first thing in the morning when she opens her laptop to check her messages from all over the world, finding responses to her blatant seductions. Seeing a new message makes her heart skip beats. The obsession continues. It was a game she realized false in its pretenses, but one Simone knew how to play well. Someone cared for her, or so it seemed. Simone needed this validation in the desperation of her loneliness. One day, two days, maybe three and the beautiful woman of her dreams usually disappeared as quickly as she emerged. Simone's heart would descend. Falling deep into the abandoned well dried up from years of loveless drought. The thump of landing on the cement bottom hurt hard and cracked the soft insides of her being.

"I'm done!" She yelled one day on one of her walks in the woods talking to the trees.

"I give up. My dating memberships expire this week. I'm not renewing."

Tears flowed down her cheeks as it started to rain accentuating her pathetic, dismal state.

Drenched, she walked back home. Her little storybook cottage in the tiny town of Pierrola in the Pacific Northwest surrounded by native land and cedars soaring high in the air, a vastness encompassing each tree.

"Ah, finally I'm home," she blurted out loud breathing in the sweet smell. "I don't want anyone else's smells, anyway," she said, hoping to console herself with her own words, letting herself be her own best company.

She ascended the spiral staircase to the top of the turret into the bathroom adjoining her bedroom. Taking her wet clothes off she stared at herself in the half mirror. Looking into her eyes, finding comfort in their darkness, their sultry depth. She looked at her breasts and folded her hands around the softness. Feeling the contours, the smoothness, and the velvety texture that was hers. A pulsating flow of energy took hold of her body, as her nipples became deliciously hard inviting more touch. She moved to the bed and let the fingers of her left hand continue this dance on her nipples alternating between gentle swirls and pulling and squeezing hard as her right hand stroked and released a pool of wetness between her legs. Her sorrow vanished, as she thought of nothing else but pleasing herself. The heat in her body surged as her whole being screamed out for touch. Her two fingers inside now, stroking and thrusting and circling in rhythm with her moans as she let herself come to the pulses of her wailing, contentment flowing into her most tender places.

Her body, a vessel for love in many forms, quieted as Simone began to feel cold. She put on her robe feeling the soft fabric envelop her. She descended to the kitchen, put the kettle on making herself a cup of lemon ginger tea and curled up on her sofa staring outside. It was dark outside when she realized she had sat there until the sun went down and she couldn't see the trees.

In the darkened room on her iPod, she began listening to Sia sing *Breathe Me,* over and over.

"Yes, just hold me," Simone repeated out loud. "Find me. Please find me. I am ready for you. I am finally ready."

She put aside her addictions. She got to the heart of her desires, wanting and needing and ready for another to love her. She felt energy release itself into the universe, felt it taking form letting it evolve as it ventured on its journey to meet that woman who was open to her. She was ready to hold the energy in her hands and feel its warm glow.

She felt ready for something real.

The next week demanded all her attention at work with more than the usual share of crises. She was known for her expertise in managing every imaginable challenge. Relaxed and knowledgeable, each day she would saunter into work meeting the anxious stares of her colleagues with her own gentle eyes. Instantly a state of calm would ensue in her place of work, a child development center. Crying children would stop crying when they saw Simone's face. Warring teachers would drop their swords when their beloved Supervisor entered their classrooms. Smiling and caring, listening to whatever was up that day. There was always something up each day. That was a given, and Simone was acutely aware that during the week she was the giver, the listener, the healer. Friday evenings were a welcome balm for her tired soul.

On that Saturday morning, as the welcoming sun filtered through her windows she woke up refreshed and rolled over in bed. Finding peace in the notion of a Saturday with nowhere to go. She opened her laptop and squinted her eyes. There was a notice indicating she had a pending message. She clicked her mouse. A note appeared advising her membership had expired, and renewal was required to read the pending message.

"Damn it. I am not doing this again! I will not find my woman online."

And with that, she slammed her computer shut. She went into the shower and let the hot water sink into her pores. She needed to get out of the house today and needed to not get on her computer. She felt the pull to renew and remembered that dating sites know how to suck you in and get your money. She felt another hint of seduction dribble through her. The game of seduction, her addiction coming alive again as she felt her nipples hardening as the water flowed down her chest. She left the shower.

Simone cracked some eggs mixing them with cinnamon and dipped her dry bread while heating the pan. She dropped in butter and spread it around letting the smells coupled with cinnamon create a delectable invitation to her senses, her mouth already watering. It's Saturday morning and a whole day to myself starting with my favorite breakfast. She poured a healthy serving of maple syrup over the cooked bread and sat down closing her eyes tasting each bite as if it was the most delicious gift from the gods. She imagined her sweetheart feeding her French toast, taking her tongue and swirling it in her mouth as they savored the maple syrup and the cinnamon together.

"Okay, I will do it." With maple syrup still on her tongue, she entered her credit card info and renewed her membership. She held her breath as the profile of the sender came into view. With her exhale she stared at the picture of a brown haired woman with mysterious dark eyes seemingly gazing into Simone's. The message popped up, and she clicked it open. It read,

"I love your face. I honestly don't know how or where to begin. It's funny, but I see your soul through your eyes. I know I'm from New Zealand so far away but please don't dismiss me. For months I have been drawn to your photo and the rich descriptions in your profile. The openness I feel towards you is unsettling and yet you feel so familiar to me. I have so much to share with you. I would do anything to look into your eyes, to kiss your face."

"PS. Listen to Fields of Gold. Eva Cassidy."

"Oh, My. God." Simone blurted out. While a voice inside of her screamed, write her back. Now.

The written words came flowing out of her.

"Yes, my beautiful goddess. We will walk hand in hand together in fields of gold. Our spirits are meeting across continents trand oceans. We will moan with delight when our hand's touch and our eyes connect, to the depths of our souls by this energy and passion between us. Let us be lost in each other as long as we want to. It is being found, not lost, our hearts connected on this newly discovered mountain of ours.

Let us hold each other here in this dream, in our story, in the depths of emotions that are filling us."

Shaking, Simone pressed send and stepped outside. Watching the leaves change color her body on fire now, knowing that in one moment an entire life can change. She noticed a stirring inside she had never experienced before. All at once she realized what a phony she had been for all this time. This new contrast was stunning her senses.

Finishing her cup of tea, she raced back to her computer finding the darkened subject line indicating a new message.

"Dearest Simone. Our energies create something that is powerful, seductive. That kindles fires of long ago and fires we have yet to make. Our spirits have aligned in such wonder and joy in these beautiful, amazing early moments. It takes my breath away. I am lost in you, in your essence, on this mountain of ours. There is nothing else I want other than this. I close my eyes and think of your words, deeply touching places inside of me that feel protected and ancient. XXX, Rachel."

Simone wrote back.

"Rachel—I am walking in fields of gold with you arm in arm. We are laughing as the wind rushes through your hair and the sun radiates through our beings, our perfect gold sun. I traveled many continents and endless oceans to find you. I thought I lost you. I cried endlessly trying to find my way to you, thinking there was no longer a path. The skies opened and light so bright it nearly blinded me came out of a vision I had. In it, you were there, you and the fire that you breathe that I inhale, a flame that illuminates even the darkest moments in life. This force connects us no matter where we are. This field of gold, these thousand years we have known each other, this breath of ours that is so sacred."

Ten minutes later another message arrived from Rachel.

"My darling, our energies have collided with such stunning intensity. Every one of my senses wants you. I am holding you with more love and tenderness than I've ever felt. I know you are holding me with love, care, and strength. This that has overcome longing and loss yet still stands open and ready to love again. Knowing this is a perfect love right here and now. Resonating with all the hopes and dreams that have always been there. I invite you to describe everything you feel, to acknowledge, to release, to embrace, to surrender, and step into this place filled with everything you have ever wanted. My arms are waiting for you only. I will always envelop whatever you wish to share. I will look tenderly into your eyes as you feel and cry and let go. As I gently kiss your forehead and continue to gaze at you as your friend, as your lover. I will hold you, dear Simone, as you relax and feel safe in my arms. XXX Rachel."

Simone had a week off from work. For the entire week, she and Rachel exchanged letters, words, and feelings. As never experienced before, these feelings completely consumed Simone. They stayed connected despite time differences. There was no sleep, as day and night merged into one.

On the Saturday of that whirlwind week, there was no letter from Rachel. On Sunday morning, there was a brief note.

"Simone. My ex came back into my life last night. Simone, we want to work things out. Please forgive me. What you and I had this past week was the most amazing thing I could ever imagine. I am lost and confused. I don't know what else to say. I know you are hurting as you read this. I hate this is hurting you. Please understand. I need some space to figure things out."

Simone stared at the computer screen, stunned.

And then the tears came. An entire day of them where she was imagining doing all kinds of terrible things to herself for being so stupid and to Rachel for being even more stupid.

The next day back at work she was in a fog. She rushed through her day. On the way home, she stopped at the beach to sit and think. A bald eagle flew overhead. It's wingspan immense, grace in its effortless soaring.

Her thoughts turned to her list of lesbian dating sites. She knew she had to find the right one. Someone was waiting for her.

Intuitively she knew she had to find Rachel.

Racing to get home she turned on her laptop zooming to the Lesboclassifieds site. She scrolled down a bit as a post caught her attention.

"Help!" it read. "The woman who was to care for my home and my three dogs, and two cats in Auckland while I go on holiday had an emergency. Is there anyone out there who can step in from this Saturday for a fortnight? Generous pay. Please love animals. They are all gentle beings that will love you instantly. Contact me ASAP if you can do this."

"Oh, my God," Simone shrieked out loud. "Rachel is in Auckland!"

"Hello." She wrote. "I would love to care for your home and your loving pets. I adore dogs and cats. I'm responsible with excellent references. Please contact me. Simone."

Two minutes later, there was a message in her inbox. Two hours later Simone had booked a round trip ticket to Auckland. Two days later she had arranged to take her accrued vacation dates. Two days after that she found her seat on United Airlines nonstop from Seattle to Auckland, New Zealand.

From the moment she got on the plane to the time it landed fifteen hours later, Simone slept. She realized she hadn't slept at all for a week. Her body caved into overwhelming exhaustion. When she woke up, the plane was circling the stunning mountains and valleys that reminded her of *The Hobbit*. She felt giddiness, she had never felt before. Somehow, she sensed she was flying home.

Upon landing, she hailed a taxi to 888 Kookaburra Street. As the car maneuvered rush hour traffic in this dazzling city, she couldn't help remember the song she had learned so many years ago. "Laugh, kookaburra, laugh kookaburra, gay your life must be!"

As she arrived at 888, the owner was ready to leave.

"You must be Simone. How lovely to meet you! I had an unexpected change in plans. I must go to the airport immediately. Perhaps your taxi driver can take me? It's all there, all the instructions and information. The money is in the envelope on the table. Thank you!"

Simone entered the palatial house as three dogs, and two cats greeted her. They sniffed and rubbed themselves against her as they bonded.

"Well hello, everyone. I am your new Mary Poppins all the way from America. Now, I have been sitting for some time, and I could use a good walk. Which of you would care to join me?"

All three dogs looked at Simone. She noticed the leashes were right by the door. Carefully she put one on each dog and stepped outside into the balmy spring day. Loving the sun on her shoulders, she let go of the autumn chill she left behind in the Pacific Northwest.

She traipsed down the street as if she had done this before. Simone felt enraptured by the cacophony of noisy birds in this otherwise quiet Auckland suburb. She had a sublime sense as if she were between the hemispheres. Suddenly she remembered she had closed the front door and forgot to take the key with her.

"Oh, merde!" she uttered in her perfect French.

Neighbors. She thought to herself. There must be a neighbor, as in next-door neighbor? A kind old lady who has the key? Oh please, I hope so, she thought.

Simone found her way back to 888 Kookaburra. With her heart beating faster than ever before she knocked on the door of 886.

She heard light footsteps from within.

The door opened, and Simone looked up. One glance was all she needed to feel a warm glow and pulsing inside of her, the intensity causing her to feel lightheaded.

She locked eyes with the stranger. Her eyes were dark, her brown hair falling around her shoulders. At that moment she felt as if her heart would stop. She'd seen this face before.

Rachel had been crying. Simone gently caressed Rachel's face, letting the tears flow onto her fingers, then licking them. Rachel grabbed her and pulled Simone to her as their hardened nipples pressed into each other. Their lips met and tongues entwined. The salt from the tears mingled with the joy on their faces.

The dogs, witnessing this miracle of fate sat

patiently waiting for this Mary Poppins to let them inside of their home, just a few feet away.

Meanwhile, Simone edged to a bench just inside the front door. The two women sat side by side, for minutes that seemed like hours. They stared at each other's faces and into each other's eyes. With each shared gaze, there was urgency for more.

"How on earth did you get here?" Rachel said.

"Mmmm. Fate. I'm not sure what else it could be. I got locked out. I am taking care of your neighbor's home and her animals."

"Oh, my God…Here's the key. Take the dogs in and do whatever you have to do and please come right back."

Simone, not used to taking orders, experienced a determination to follow Rachel's command. Returning five minutes later, Rachel took her hand and led them to her bedroom as they reached for each other's lips. With urgency, their mouths opened, and their tongues danced in, swirling, then deeper and pulling each other closer. They couldn't get close enough as wetness poured between their legs. Their lips and tongues and hands expressed the fire between them.

Rachel's lips kept finding Simone's as this pull towards each other ignited. Their lips craved more as their hands wrapped them into a folding embrace. Buttons unbuttoned, lips touched skin, and wetness glistened between them. Hands caressed, as more snaps and zippers released skin, letting the softness between them surge into a frenzied display of desire. In their minds, each thought why us? Of all the forces in the universe from one hemisphere to another we found each other, we merge. They moaned and came together. The heat grew between them as their bodies screamed for more. The hunger between two strangers waiting a lifetime for each other was satisfied.

A blissful quiet ensued as they held each other... crying, loving, feeling safe, feeling full. As sleep glided into the empty spaces, the women folded into each other. They were a perfect fit as they sunk into the luscious bed with a night of happy dreams into the light of day.

When they woke up, the sun was streaming through the windows, glittering and reflecting rainbows around them from the glass crystals hanging from the window frame.

"Mmmmm," Simone murmured. Suddenly remembering, she whispered, "Your ex?"

"Done. Kiss me. Now."

Simone leaned into Rachel mixing fire with sublime, as the kiss took on a life of its own. Her breath quickened as she felt herself swoon. She pinned Rachel down, her thighs wet from the intensity of desire. Her body slid over Rachel's. She moved down her curves with the grace of a dancer in full control of her stage, as Rachel writhed underneath her skin scorching and slippery, her moans accompanying this endless dance. Simone arrived playfully and without forgiveness to her lover's labia. She tasted her thrusting ever so gently at first, and then circling following Rachel's moans with her tongue and her fingers, squeezing the hardness of her nipples as Rachel screamed. Simone wouldn't stop. She was starving for her screams as she pressed into Rachel, her tongue, her hands, and Rachel's aftershocks exploding with one last gasp. Then a moment of quiet, of serenity in this, the sublime.

Minutes turned to hours. Time had no meaning, no direction, as the two women studied each other.

Noticing all the little nuances, the perfections, and the imperfections, their eyes, the windows to a being shining with such love. They wanted more. They liked what they saw, their smiles conveying a message of kindness, of acceptance, of desire. All words ceased as their eyes beckoned their bodies for more, the merging of two beings.

Rachel grazed her lips over Simone's feeling at home. As she tenderly caressed those lips finding urgency for more as her desire unleashed. Her mouth was on Simone's nipples, soft then hardened, beckoning intensity. She stayed there at the breasts of her lover, kissing every contour, loving every part of her. She wrapped her legs around Simone letting the juices flow between them as together they writhed in their pure element of love and desire. In their passion, a final moan sent them laughing and crying as they wrapped around each other tenderly, like two presents gifted from the universe.

Simone fell into a satiated sleep. After stroking the beauty cascading around her, Rachel slipped away to tend to the animals next door.

Six hours later in the late afternoon, Simone's eyes opened.

"Tell me what you are feeling my darling, tell me." Rachel's hand was gently stroking Simone's face, as Simone looked into her eyes, feeling tears well up.

"I feel like I am home. When I look at you, into you, I have that feeling of a sigh, a breath of life that never ends. I am home. I felt it the moment you opened the door yesterday. I know that my next journey in life begins with you. This truth is pulsing through me. I can't go back. I don't want to take a plane back to the U.S. in two weeks. It might seem crazy since we just met, but I just know we are meant to be together."

"No, it's not crazy. I don't want you to get on that plane, either. You belong here. Our hearts have decided this." They laughed as their lips met again, sealing the declaration.

Simone felt a surging warm glow inside of her as she embraced this magic around her. She knew the woman next to her was her destiny, these bridges connecting their souls from their separate lives to the stunning beauty that is now their present. Coming from one hemisphere to another, profoundly she felt like she was home.

They grabbed each other rolling on the bed, kissing again and laughing in their newfound joy.

For the next two weeks, they shared two homes, one with animals to care for and one for themselves. Rachel called the office of her architect firm and told her secretary she would be on holiday for a while, allowing her full self to simply be with this woman who was now her life, who had become her fire, her mirror, her companion, her hopes and her dreams.

For both Simone and Rachel, this was the beginning of an awakening. Of finding with each other passion they never knew existed. Each day and into the nights their lovemaking took on a life of its own, starvation, a fire between them surging and enveloping them, asking and begging for release. In true love with another, there is an infinite amount of passion, of longing, of loving from the body and soul, from the very place that wants and needs to merge with one's other half. The two women entered each other's hearts and beings. They knew this was just the beginning and they were living a love story that might have begun lifetimes ago. These two women were destined for love, and knowing this they were able to breathe deeply and relax into each other.

As they were holding each other tenderly Simone whispered into Rachel's ear, "You know…Hmm…"

Rachel responded, moving on top of Simone, looking into her eyes, kissing her nose, her eyelids, her cheeks, her lips.

"Will you marry me?"

"Oh, my God, yes. Yes! Yes! Yes," said Simone.

This love gives forth the newness of two people finding each other.

Emerald has written three children's books, a novel, countless short stories and essays, creative non-fiction short pieces and a full-length memoir. She is in the process of writing her second and third novels. In each of these pieces, she is inspired by words, by relationships, by cultures and society, by feelings and the human heart, and by the earth we all live in.

Sixteen Years Overdue

Aila Boyd

Alison sat alone in the lavish dining room of the luxurious Boston condo she shared with her longtime fiancé and soon to be husband. Her face painted exquisitely with high-end beauty products, displayed sadness and concern. Several strategically placed candles lit the room. She was only twenty-five, and yet the lighting showed forehead wrinkles and fine lines around her eyes. She felt as if she had been waiting for ages and was about ready to call it a night, blow out the candles, and go to bed hungry despite her gurgling stomach. She could no longer smell the mouth-watering aroma of the gourmet Italian food she picked up earlier in the evening and placed carefully into plates and bowls in an attempt to pass it off as her cooking. The reserve bottle of 1982 vintage wine lost its chill and was now lukewarm.

Just as her anxiety was about to overwhelm her, she heard a faint noise coming from the other room. She listened intently, realizing someone was attempting to unlock the front door with what sounded like the wrong key? Still waiting on her soon to be husband to arrive for the romantic dinner she prepared, she walked over and looked through the peephole. Sure enough, there he was, the elusive Mr. Willie Ronald.

As she opened the door, she planned to give him a piece of her mind. Before she could, he lunged forward and planted a sloppy wet kiss on her lips—a strategy he had used in the past when he'd disappointed her.

The two eventually settled down at the table and picked at their now cold dinner, while he droned on about the office and counted off a laundry list of reasons for arriving late.

"Willie this is the last night we get to spend together before our wedding next week," she finally said, cutting him off.

"Well if it were up to me you would just stay here with me instead of spending the entire week leading up to our wedding with your bridesmaids," he mumbled in between hefty forkfuls of mushroom ravioli.

"It's a tradition, and you know that. All of my girlfriends have done the same thing. I don't want to be the one to break from the tradition."

"Heavens no!" He said,

"Did you ever talk to your boss about getting time off for a honeymoon?"

As soon as he heard the word honeymoon, Willie's entire body language shifted to a more guarded demeanor. His chewing grew slow. His eyes rolled around in search of a way to ease the blow he was about to deliver to his bride's dream of having the most exciting Irish honeymoon imaginable.

"Well…I found out I have to travel for business the day after the wedding so we might have to hold off on making any big plans," he said.

"Travel for business? We're talking about the same thing aren't we, our honeymoon? Something that is a once in a lifetime thing!" She said,

"I know, but they're sending me to this important

business meeting in Montevideo to determine if opening a new production facility is a viable option."

"Montevideo? Viable option? I think our honeymoon is more of a viable option than a production facility," she said.

"I know, sugar plum, but Uruguay will be a big get for the company, which means a big salary raise for me, which also means more money to spend shopping for you."

She paused before responding. She took a sip of the warm red wine and swished it around in her mouth as she processed her options. She came across the perfect solution to Willie's misguided commitment to his work and her need to have the honeymoon of her dreams.

"I'm coming with you," she said.

"What do you mean you're coming with me? It's a business trip."

"I'll go with you to Uruguay, and you'll go to your business meeting as planned. When you finish your business, meet me, and we'll spend a few days at some lovely little tropical resort town on the coast. It's settled," Alison said.

⁂

Ms. Cheyenne Justice's art classroom at Baldwin Briggs Elementary School in Abilene, Texas was littered with empty pizza boxes, half eaten bags of chips, and juice boxes. The atmosphere in the room was joyous as her advanced art class celebrated the end of the school year and the masterful pieces of art created under the loving guidance of Ms. Justice. It was apparent from the way she interacted with her students that she enjoyed them and her job. Keeping with annual tradition, she required her students to place their art projects in a giant display case at the front of the room for everyone to observe and appreciate. At the end of the year, she allowed students to take their pieces home with them or have them remain in the room as part of the permanent display. As much as she enjoyed getting to see the look of excitement and pride on her student's faces when they took the art home to show their parents, it genuinely pained her. She no longer had the pleasure of seeing all of the beautiful art that her students worked so carefully to create during the school year.

Making her way to the front of the room, she brushed her hands through her short hair. The apron wrapped tightly around her torso was once flawlessly white. After years of art classes, it was now every color of the rainbow.

"Attention! Attention my little artists," she called out in an upbeat inflection as she waved her hands high above her head.

As if they were perfectly conditioned, all of the students stopped what they were doing and gave her their undivided attention.

"I just wanted to tell you guys that you rocked this year, like the little Picassos you are. I want every one of you to keep up the good work over the summer. Remember, you don't have to be in school to paint a beautiful picture or to draw a realistic portrait. Am I right?"

Immediately the students echoed back that she was right, sounding as if they were at a pep rally instead of an elementary school art classroom.

"What are you going to do this summer Ms.

Justice?" asked a little girl in the front of the room who had cropped brown hair and was missing one of her two front teeth.

"What am I going to do this summer? Why I'm going exploring of course!"

"Where," asked the little girl?

"Uruguay," she shouted with excitement. "Does anyone know where Uruguay is?"

Looks of confusion filled the faces of her students.

"South America, of course!"

As soon as she said South America, the students erupted into an excited concert of squeals, followed by an assortment of questions about the culture and the type of people who are native to the small South American country.

⊰⊹⊱

Alison arrived in Maldonado, a quaint coastal town in the southeastern part of Uruguay, alone in a chauffeured car. She was hesitant to leave her new husband just a day after their blissful wedding ceremony was plastered all over the social pages of *The Boston Globe*. Alison agreed to be driven to the hotel after Willie assured her he would join her in two days. She looked out the window of her sleek black town car in awe of the views. Alison's first trip to South America left her feeling excited. She was so wrapped up in the sights of a new country and a place that capsulated all of her tropical fantasies, she spent little time fretting over being alone.

⊰⊹⊱

Immediately after Cheyenne checked into the luxurious twelve story hotel that cost her half a month's salary for her weeklong stay, she rushed out of the lobby and inhaled a giant breath of South Atlantic Ocean air. She had been dreaming of visiting Uruguay since she first read *Evohe* by Christina Peri Rossi while taking a women's studies course at Texas State University. The impact that Rossi's poetry had on her, since her time as a young coed was undeniable. Standing in Rossi's country of origin was a moment she'd never forget. It was Rossi's writings that had dramatically shaped the early days of Cheyenne's coming to terms with her sexuality. Having not dipped her toes into anything deeper than a country creek since she visited the Gulf of Mexico with her parents as a child, Cheyenne desperately wanted to visit a beach. She was suddenly overcome by an unexpected childlike desire to throw herself down on the ground and roll back and forth on the pristine white sandy coastline. She managed to restrain herself and pulled herself away from the water's edge long enough to locate her first-floor room, which was modest compared to the majority of the other rooms in the hotel. It was hers and hers alone for a week.

※ ※ ※ ※

After having spent nearly an hour in one of the indoor Jacuzzis in an attempt to avoid unwarranted sun exposure to her ivory Scotch-Irish complexion, Alison stepped out onto the balcony, with only an oversized plush towel wrapped around her petite body. She delicately laid out her floral one-piece bathing suit to dry on the white railing that separated her from a twelve-story fall to the ground below. Just as Alison started to turn around to go into her room for a mid-afternoon nap, a gust of wind swooped up the bathing suit, causing it to fall to the ground below. Horrified that her sopping wet bathing suit had just flown away, she quickly leaned over the railing and looked down to see that her bathing suit had fallen onto a woman who was stretched out on a lounge chair, soaking up the blistering warmth of the Uruguayan summer day. Cheyenne had been asleep when the bathing suit first landed on her chest but was quickly startled awake, confused by what had just happened.

"Oh my God. I'm sorry." Alison yelled down to her while waving her hands in the air.

Cheyenne immediately saw the humor in the situation and offered to return the bathing suit to her after noticing that Alison had already undressed and wasn't decent enough to take a stroll down to the pool. Alison graciously accepted Cheyenne's kind offer and yelled down to her that she was in the penthouse.

Less than five minutes later, Cheyenne knocked lightly on the set of double doors that led into the penthouse suite with the soaking wet bathing suit in hand. Alison threw open the doors, and with little reservation launched into a long-winded apology thanking Cheyenne time and time again for being so kind in returning her bathing suit.

"It's a beautiful floral print by the way," Cheyenne said as she handed the suit back to Alison, causing her to blush. "It's almost as if it's a wearable work of art."

"Oh I don't know about that," Alison said as she threw it into the bathroom sink. "I forgot to pack a bathing suit and just picked it up in the lobby gift shop."

Noticing the shower was running, Cheyenne looked to Alison and said, "Well I guess I should let you get back to your shower."

"Oh no," Alison frantically said. "I mean you can't leave…you can't leave without letting me pay you for the trouble I've caused you."

"It's no trouble," Cheyenne said. "It's no trouble at all."

As Alison turned around to reach for her purse, the towel she was wearing got caught on a table and fell to the ground, leaving Alison naked in front of a total stranger. Cheyenne knew she should look away, it was the polite thing to do, but Alison was gorgeous with a perfect body.

Without warning, Cheyenne and Alison found themselves in a passionate embrace, with their bodies smashed up against each other as their lips met and their tongues explored. The towel that covered Alison's body long forgotten. Cheyenne couldn't stop staring at Alison's body, perky round breasts, slender stomach, and the hairless, smoothness of her woman's center.

Neither of the women made a fuss over Alison's compromised state or the fact they had just met. They were caught up in each other. Alison stood confidently in all of her naked bliss as they continued to kiss and explore each other. Not wanting Cheyenne to feel excluded, Alison slowly ran her hands up Cheyenne's back until she located the strap that held her bathing suit in place. She gently worked the strap of the bathing suit over Cheyenne's head. With a swift downward jerk, the spandex suit rolled down over Cheyenne's bosom to reveal her full breasts and erect nipples. Alison paused for a moment to take in her naked breasts, prompting Cheyenne to pick up where she had left off, exposing the remainder of her older, yet equally beautiful body.

They eventually made their way into the bathroom, under the vigorous stream of the showerhead. Soaking in the steamy warmth of the shower, they took turns lathering each other's bodies. Losing track of time, they exited the shower when the warm water ceased, and the icy coldness forced them out.

⁂

Several hours later, as the sun started to retreat, Alison and Cheyenne found themselves satiated from their unplanned love making and hungry for dinner. They walked to a small seafood restaurant a couple of blocks down from the hotel that asserted its commitment to local catches on all of its advertisements. Looking at the menu, Cheyenne realized that she hadn't budgeted enough money for such a lavish meal.

"What looks good to you?" Alison asked as she waved the menu back and forth.

Cheyenne was hesitant to respond. Her eyes were darting back and forth across the menu in search of a moderately priced entrée.

"Um...I'm not sure yet. How about you?"

"The pecan crusted lobster tail sounds delicious."

Cheyenne quickly glanced over at the lobster section of the menu and was shocked to see that it came with a much heftier price tag than she had ever spent on an entire week's groceries.

"Well, I don't know. Lobster isn't really for me."

"What is for you then?" Alison asked as she fluttered her eyelashes with a giddy smile.

"You," Cheyenne slowly purred as she nudged Alison's feet under the table.

Alison paused for a minute then said, "Whatever you want. It's all on me."

"Oh no! I couldn't possibly. Please, let me."

Just then the waiter walked over and asked if they were ready to order or if they needed more time with the menu. Alison abruptly took hold of Cheyenne's menu and handed them both over to the waiter.

"We'll both have the lobster and your best bottle of wine," she said with a smooth conviction.

Cheyenne's face instantly showed concern as she waved off the waiter.

"Oh no. You don't have to do that, Alison."

Feeling as if they were on the verge of popping from their scrumptious dinner and wine, they slowly found their way onto the sandy shores in the early hours of the night. The moon illuminated the calmness of the low tide. They walked until the lavish meal was a distant memory. The later it got, the fewer people they met along their waterfront stroll. When they finally were alone, they sneaked a quick kiss before splashing through the water's edge. They spent the rest of the night into dawn in Alison's room making love.

❧❧❧❧❧

The next morning, after returning to her room in the early hours of the morning, Cheyenne got dressed and took the elevator up to the twelfth floor to Alison's penthouse suite. She eagerly waited as the elevator slowly climbed to the top floor of the hotel. She imagined what Alison might look like this morning. An image of tousled hair and glowing skin came to mind, an image that very much excited her.

She quickly gave the door several knocks,

assuming that Alison might still be asleep, but was surprised when the door opened no more than a second or two later. Cheyenne's anticipation shifted to shock. There stood a man in his boxers, looking at Cheyenne with a slightly puzzled expression. "May I help you?" he asked.

"Um…I must have the wrong room," she said, attempting to make sense of a half-naked man in Alison's room.

In the distance, Alison's voice seeped out into the hallway where Cheyenne stood dumbfounded. She frantically leaned back and forth, attempting to look past this man to catch a glimpse of Alison.

Unable to suppress the urge, she yelled "Alison? Alison? Are you in there?"

Willie felt instantly alarmed as this strange woman in this foreign country yelled out his wife's name. He grabbed hold of the door and tried to slam it shut. Before he could, Alison emerged alongside him in the doorway.

"Cheyenne…oh there you are," Alison acknowledged coyly.

Cheyenne's eyes grew larger by the minute as she stepped back and sized up the situation, intently studying the man and wife that stood before her as she said, "And who is this?"

"Oh, silly me, Cheyenne. This is my husband, Willie. Willie, this is Cheyenne. She's a guest at the hotel. I met her down by the pool yesterday," Alison relayed to the two puzzled individuals looking to her for answers. It was apparent that Alison was attempting to consider both sides of the situation, as she tried to avoid upsetting either one of them.

"Uh, nice to meet you," Willie said to Cheyenne

as he extended his hand. "We're getting ready to go out for breakfast, care to join us?"

"That's a lovely idea, dear. Yes please join us," Alison said to Cheyenne, trying to reach out to her.

Cheyenne reluctantly agreed and said she would reserve a table at the hotel restaurant while the seemingly happy couple finished getting ready. Cheyenne ordered a bowl of fruit and black coffee, while Alison and Willie decided to split a breakfast sampler of eggs, bacon, sausage, pancakes, and an assortment of muffins. After they ordered, Willie droned on about his meeting going better than planned. Willie assured Alison he was glad that she so adamantly pushed them to use this business trip for their honeymoon.

The word honeymoon caught Cheyenne off-guard. She felt slapped by his words. The reality was starting to hit her as she imagined Alison and Willie exchanging their vows in some romantic New England ceremony, a notion that currently disgusted her. Visibly angered, Cheyenne was shocked by the news of Alison's recent marriage to Willie, one she'd failed to mention the previous day. Alison attempted to distract Willie from any talks of their marriage or honeymoon. Despite that, he rambled on for most of the breakfast as he relived the details of their wedding and the cost of Ivy League educations for yet to be conceived children. He patted himself on the back for financially securing this with the promotion he will get as a reward for closing the business deal in Montevideo on their honeymoon.

After consuming more than half of the sampler, Willie excused himself to the little boy's room, leaving Alison and Cheyenne alone for the first time since the previous night. Alison immediately thrust herself into a heartfelt apology, explaining that she had meant to tell her about Willie, but she was so swept up in the excitement of yesterday that it slipped her mind. This apology was one Cheyenne wasn't planning on accepting.

"We agreed to go windsurfing today! Did you just happen to forget about your new husband or did you plan for the three of us to go?" Cheyenne asked with seething anger.

"He wasn't supposed to come down until tomorrow," Alison pleaded. "Please forgive me."

Willie finally returned to the table, oblivious to the conversation that had taken place while he was absent. While he was ordering another mimosa from the flirtatious waitress, Cheyenne offered a sly wink to Alison, a wink that was eagerly received.

❧❦❧❦

Over the next several days Cheyenne repeatedly called up to the penthouse suite, only to be greeted by the automated voice of the answering machine. Each morning and afternoon she would ride the elevator up to the penthouse and knock on the door, each time preparing for Willie to answer the door. No one answered. She knew that if she could get a few moments alone with Alison, they could hash the whole thing out and she might be able to enjoy her remaining vacation. Her desire to see Alison grew with each unanswered attempt.

Meanwhile, Alison was out from sunrise to sunset with Willie exploring the local scene and engaging in a wide assortment of fun activities that neither one of them would have ever dreamed of doing back in the cozy comforts of their day-to-day lives. Every night when they returned to the room, Alison saw they had several missed calls and no voicemail messages. Alison knew that Cheyenne had been calling, but she couldn't manage to find more than a few seconds away from Willie. After spending thirty grueling minutes on his cell phone interrupting Alison and Willie's snorkeling lesson, Willie reluctantly informed Alison he had to go back to work in the States. The company was itching to move forward on his Uruguayan advances. They needed him back in the USA office immediately. Alison and Willie agreed to leave Uruguay the following morning.

That night Alison sneaked away after Willie dozed off early from drinking too many local beers. She knocked on Cheyenne's door. From the expression on her face, Cheyenne appeared surprised, yet thrilled to see Alison. Alison explained to Cheyenne the many reasons why she hadn't been able to return her calls and that she and Willie would be leaving the country the following morning. The news caused Cheyenne to become visibly distraught. Alison assured Cheyenne that she wanted to stay in contact as she handed her a sheet of paper with her phone number scribbled on it. Almost instinctually, Alison leaned in to kiss Cheyenne, as Cheyenne pulled back with a solemn look on her face.

"What's wrong?" Alison asked.

"I just can't, Alison, now that I know you're married. You should go back and be with your husband."

Alison reluctantly exited Cheyenne's room.

Less than a week before the new school year was scheduled to start, Cheyenne received word from the school board. They were transferring her to a high school position for a grade level she had never taught before. The school wasn't just any high school. It was the most notorious high school in the district, known for its horrendous disciplinary issues and low testing scores. The entire summer passed, and Cheyenne never dialed the number that Alison had given her. The closer the first day of school got, the more frequently Cheyenne looked at the phone number and contemplated whether or not to dial it. Finally, on the night before the first day of school, she broke her silence and dialed Alison's phone number. She was pleased when Alison answered on the first ring.

"Hello. Who is this?" Alison said in a tone of voice that sounded alien to Cheyenne, nothing close to the way she remembered it from the time that they spent in Uruguay together.

"Alison? Alison, it's me, Cheyenne," she said, hoping for an ecstatic response.

Upon realizing who it was, Alison greeted her and asked how she was doing. The conversation went on for roughly fifteen minutes until Cheyenne felt compelled to go beyond the friendly chatter that dominated their conversation thus far. Something seemed off with the woman who she remembered so clearly.

"What's wrong, Alison? You don't sound like yourself over the phone," Cheyenne said.

She waited for a response, wondering if Alison might have hung up on her. "I've been blessed with a baby Cheyenne. Willie and I are having a baby," she said with a shaky voice that lacked an ounce of conviction or excitement over the revelation.

❧ ❧ ❧ ❧

After that call, Cheyenne and Alison's phone conversations continued on a daily basis, into the early hours of the morning. Cheyenne would tell Alison how horrible her day was at the new high school and how she wished she could go back to teaching in an elementary school. After Alison gave birth, she rarely left her apartment, often relying on her conversations with Cheyenne for communication with the outside world. Their daily conversations went on for years. Neither one of them dared to suggest they meet in person. Secretly they both held onto the idea of recreating the magical time they experienced together that fateful summer in Uruguay. They both feared that meeting in person again might ruin the connection they both treasured dearly. After only one year of teaching art in the new high school position, Cheyenne tendered her letter of resignation at the urging of Alison so that she could fulfill her lifelong dream of opening her art gallery, a gallery that she filled exclusively with paintings and drawings of her creation. Although it was nothing more than a tiny hole in the wall that sat several blocks off the main street, the gallery was hers, and it meant almost as much to her as her daily conversations with Alison.

❧ ❧ ❧ ❧

After Sixteen years of daily phone conversations, Alison called Cheyenne early one morning. Mornings were Cheyenne's most creative period of the day, and Alison never called during this time. Alison's voice was shaky, and she sounded unsure of herself.

"What's wrong, Alison? Please don't tell me you caught the flu from Willie or Jackson," Cheyenne said, referencing Alison's fifteen-year old son.

"Willie…he's been cheating on me for over eight months," she said with zero emotion.

The news hit Cheyenne like a brick wall. Although she envied the fact that Willie was married to Alison and she wasn't, she had grown to appreciate him since their joint breakfast that morning years earlier. The news devastated her in a way that she would have never predicted.

"I have to get out of Boston," Alison proclaimed.

"You could always come visit me," Cheyenne said, unsure whether or not she had crossed the line.

"No. I've decided that Jackson and I are moving."

"Moving where?" Cheyenne said.

"Maldonado Uruguay," said Alison.

The word Maldonado shocked Cheyenne, having not heard the word spoken out loud in years. They stayed on the phone for hours that day, longer than they normally did, debating whether such a move would be practical. Alison stood by her decision and wouldn't budge.

"Oh my God! If I'm going, then you have to go with me," Alison exclaimed, as the notion fully materialized in her mind.

Cheyenne took a ragged breath as images of the quaint, picturesque town flashed through her mind with the speed of a strobe light.

꧁꧂꧁꧂

Two months later, Alison and Jackson, a tall

and lanky young man, met Cheyenne at the airport in Montevideo. Cheyenne had already been in the country for several weeks and drove up from the small waterfront apartment she had been renting in Maldonado. They had originally planned to arrive in the country at the same time. However, it took slightly longer than anticipated finalizing her divorce from Willie.

Their reunion was one of joy and comfort, having spent so many years apart. For the first several minutes they simply gazed at each other in disbelief that they were finally back where it had all started.

"Aren't you going to say something?" Jackson asked his mother with a sly expression etched across his face.

Although his mother never directly explained to him who Cheyenne was, Jackson knew their connection was more than friends.

Alison quickly wrapped her arms around Cheyenne's neck and squeezed her tightly. She then smashed her lips up against Cheyenne's in a passionate kiss. They felt as wonderfully supple as she'd remembered.

As they slowly pulled back from each other, Cheyenne said, "Sometimes actions do speak louder than words."

"In our case it did," said Alison while placing another light kiss on Cheyenne's lips.

All three of them laughed for a moment, while an awkward silence quickly set in as they looked at each other.

Taking hold of Jackson's forearm, Alison said, "I want you to meet my son."

Jackson extended his hand in an attempt to

greet Cheyenne with a formal shake. She immediately swatted his arm away and embraced him in a warm hug.

That afternoon the three of them went house hunting with the money that Alison received in the divorce settlement. After touring a promising house on the outskirts of town, Jackson turned to them and asked, "Can I have the master bedroom?" Cheyenne and Alison looked at each other and started laughing.

"We're in paradise, sure why not," Cheyenne proclaimed, and Alison wholeheartedly agreed.

Aila Boyd is a Virginia based writer and award-winning journalist. She holds an M.F.A. in writing from Lindenwood University.

Separate Huts

By Sallyanne Monti

I'm groggy and disoriented. I roll over in the unfamiliar bed searching for the bright red numbers on the bedside alarm clock—5:30 a.m. *No jet lag*, I think to myself while noting my usual wake-up time despite yesterday's cross-country plane flight.

I just came off an all women cruise to the Bahamas with a well-known lesbian travel company. Up until a few days ago, I was their resident DJ, traveling around the world several weeks per month playing music for the ladies on their all-women vacations. I flew to Seattle yesterday to accept an OutMusic Award for best LGBT DJ, held at the Seattle Repertory Theatre. The event featured the who's who in music entertainment. The award was an honor and a culmination of accolades for decades of service to the LGBT community.

I rub my eyes, run my fingers through my curly brown shoulder length hair and raise my hands over my head. I grab hold of the wooden slats of the headboard behind me while stretching my legs straight out. Pointing my toes at the TV mounted on the wall in front of me, I let out a slow moan, releasing the tension through my stretch while raising both legs towards the ceiling and rocking my hips upward. I smile as I feel my lower back pop. *Who needs a Chiropractor when you have wake-up stretches?* I look around the room wishing there was a coffee maker and remember the lobby had a complimentary beverage station. I grunt thinking *if you call a thermos of coffee and tiny Styrofoam cups a beverage station?*

I decided to hide out from the media in the last place anyone would think to find me. The low-end motel was a clean, safe, no-frills overnight option within a short drive to SeaTac, Seattle's international airport that would take me far away from the love of my life. I will join the Bora Bora all-inclusive Resort Team in the Tahitian Islands as their exclusive DJ, where I can continue to wallow in the loss of my three-year relationship with Carly Dobbs. I hadn't seen Carly in over two years, and yet the memories of her were painful and very much alive.

Tomorrow I'll start a new life—alone, heartbroken and distracted, in Bora Bora. Today, coffee and lots of it was definitely in order. I'm in Seattle, the coffee capital of the world. After my initial lobby caffeine fix, I'll head out in search of some real java.

I sit up and jump out of bed, removing my nightshirt and undies while dropping them onto the bottom of the bed. I head naked to the bathroom as I unceremoniously trip over the chair leg protruding into the small walkway between the end of the bed and the makeshift desk next to the television. I hold my right foot in my hand rubbing my pinky toe while hopping the remaining few feet to the bathroom.

Glad I'd unpacked the few essentials the night before. I take stock of my toothbrush, toothpaste and travel size hair products lying next to the tiny bar of wrapped soap with the motel's logo. As I lean over the toilet, I reach into the bathtub and turn on the shower water letting it cascade between my fingers while waiting for it to go from cold to hot. Satisfied with the water temperature, I withdraw my arm as the vinyl shower curtain immediately sticks to my wrist on the way out. I violently shake my entrapped hand in an attempt to free myself, while encasing my entire arm in plastic.

"Fuck, shit and fuck again," I mutter while wondering how many dirty naked travelers had been entangled in this disgusting shower sarong, leaving microscopic traces of their DNA behind. Grossed out and suddenly cranky, I grab the end of the shower curtain with my free hand and yank it to the other side of the tub as the white plastic peels off of my arm and sticks to itself like a piece of plastic wrap gone wrong. As I step into the tub, the shower curtain promptly sticks to my ass. At that moment, as I reach behind me in an incensed attempt to free myself, I burst into tears.

With no warning, my memory assaults me. I'm no longer at the motel in Seattle. I'm in another hotel at another place and another time—right back there, with her, my heart—my darling Carly, the love of my life—my person.

We were naked and frenzied in that shower as we grabbed for each other in the powerful cascade of water. Our bodies shimmering in soapy water as we pressed against each other, getting as close as we could, our centers gyrating in unison. I closed my eyes as her mouth slammed into my lips, her tongue meeting mine in a frantic attempt to connect on every level. We held each other tight rocking back and forth and then side-to-side, moaning and shouting above the sound of the flowing water.

"I love you my darling

I love you too, so much," she replied.

Don't ever leave me, baby."
"I never will," she said.
And I believed her.

Suddenly we were unable to move, almost frozen in place. So engrossed in each other, it took us several minutes to realize *the hotel's utilitarian shower curtain swathed us in a slimy vinyl cocoon.*

The water turned cold, jolting me back into the lonely reality of the motel shower. As I rubbed my hands over the tears streaming down my face in the spray of the now icy water, I reminded myself that Carly had never truly been mine. She made it clear from the start that we'd never share the same home, never live together, never be a cohabitated us, and we'd always live in separate huts as she put it. To her, this was a joke, a funny contradiction of our needs. To me, it was devastation, an excision of my desperate need to live together. Need I would never see fulfilled.

This irreconcilable difference became a source of contention for our loosely defined and complicated us. We'd been together for three years, and I hadn't seen Carly in two years. At the drop of memory, she was right back here with me. A reminder of all the ways I'd begged her to be like me, a reminder of all the ways she could only be the way she was, holding me at a distance. Had it been two years since I held her in my arms since we parted ways in an irreconcilable difference of her cohabitation phobia and my cohabitation obsession?

We met at the Burbank Airport, five years ago. I remember the details as if it were yesterday. As my plane landed, I made my way to the front of the aircraft walking down the steps onto the tarmac following the painted white lined path to the terminal door that led me to the airport gate. As I walked past the gate attendant, my head down searching in my bag for my cell phone, I tripped over my own feet propelling myself into her. My face landed between her breasts as her soft body prevented my fall. My propelling weight sent her slamming backward through the life-size cardboard cutouts of the cast of *Friends* that had been surrounding her, while her fall was broken by the wall behind her. I looked up into the smiling faces of Chandler, Joey, and Ross, and felt utterly confused as she pushed towards me steadying her balance by placing the palms of her hands firmly against my chest while splaying her fingers across my breasts. I suppose this made us even. I had just completed a swan dive into her boobs.

"Uh…Hi, my name is Rena Barton."

I slid my right hand in between our bodies in a squished attempt to encourage a handshake and to learn her name. She was dumbfounded, stunned, or suffering from shock, as she neither responded nor removed her hands from my breasts. I stared into her light gray eyes noticing the black circles highlighting her irises and speckles of green smudging through the gray. Her eyebrows were thinly shaped, their color matching the chestnut brown of her straight shoulder-length hair. She was slender and stood at my height, about five feet, five inches tall. I stepped back a bit and gently slipped my thumbs under her palms while lifting her hands from my breasts.

"I'm sorry, Ms.—?" I said.

She continued to stare saying nothing.

"Are you okay? I didn't mean to plow into you or wind up face first in your boobs."

She tried to look stern and then burst out laughing.

"I take it by that reaction you didn't mind me landing in your boobs?"

She extracted her hands from my grasp and said, "I'm Carly Dobbs, and I think I'm pleased to meet you?"

"Well, Carly Dobbs thank you for breaking my fall. Bad enough the plane delays will get me home late. I'd have a lot of explaining to do to my cat if I showed up with two black eyes."

"Oh, you have a talking cat at home?" She said,

"Well in a manner of speaking yes, he is quite the vocal kitty. He even sings."

"Sings, sings to what?"

"He sings to my music, and he's just purrfect—Okay scratch that, that was a lame joke." I smiled at her and said, "I'm a music DJ, and I create my tracks and playlists in my home studio."

"I knew you looked familiar, but couldn't place where I've seen you. What's your DJ name?"

"DJ Purrfect," I said. "And my cat's name is Barton," I added.

"Wait a minute, your professional DJ name is for your cat, and your cat's name is your real last name?" She laughed uproariously, saying, "I was sure Purrfect had more to do with the clientele you are serving and less to do with your cat, wow."

I backed up putting some space between us while reassembling the life-size cast of Friends cutouts back to their original positions. When I finished, I looked at her. She was wearing dark brown shorts, a matching shirt, and a brown sun visor.

"So what do you do for a living, UPS driver?" I asked.

"Excuse me?" she said.

By the smirk on her face and the tilt of her head, I had offended her. I looked closer and noticed that her dark brown shorts and matching dark brown button-

down shirt were lacking a UPS logo. After further scrutiny, I realized most UPS drivers didn't wear fanny packs, sun visors or penny loafers with white crew socks like she was wearing.

She watched me intently. Crossing her arms, she raised her eyebrows and began tapping her left foot.

I had some making up to do, and I better do it fast if I ever wanted to see Ms. Carly Dobbs again. I did want to see her again. I very much wanted to see her.

"So, why are you here, at the airport?" I said.

"I just flew home from a business meeting in San Francisco."

"Business?" I said.

"An annual conference, at the Moscone Center on Howard St. in Downtown."

"What kind of conference?" I asked.

"A ZumbaCon, I'm a Zumba teacher."

"You're serious?" I smiled as I shook my head from side to side.

"A Zumba teacher and a music DJ, a match made in harmony," she said.

She stuck her hand out and said, "Well Rena Barton, DJ Purrfect, I think I'll let you take me out to dinner. I expect by dessert, you'll try to talk yourself out of almost knocking me over and insulting my almost brown collar profession."

I smiled as I shook her hand and said, "Carly Dobbs it will be my pleasure."

She was everything I never thought I'd be attracted to and yet she was everything I was attracted to and more. Every minute of every day I loved her more, desired her more and wanted her more. Carly had a high-profile Zumba practice. I was a well-known DJ—both of us working in the Los Angeles scene and lesbian community across the country. We both traveled several weeks a month for work and spent the remaining time together in either of our apartments. As we approached our one-year anniversary, I asked Carly to move in with me. We had just made love. We were lying in bed naked with our legs intertwined holding hands while watching Food Network.

"I am too the better cook Carly, and you know it."

"I beg to differ. My homemade pizza leaves you breathless, and you know it, Rena."

"Okay, I will give you that. You and pizza are my weaknesses. For either, I'd do just about anything. For both, I'd give up everything in my life. Move in with me and make me the happiest woman in the world. I will worship you all the days of my life, love you like no one ever did or ever will, and be faithful to our love with every fiber of my being. You're my heart and my soul and everything that matters."

She moved her legs off of mine, let go of my hand, sat up in bed and faced me.

"Rena, you know I love you. Nothing has changed. I can't live with you. I just can't live with anyone. It's not how I'm wired. I need my space and my place to create, to be, to meditate, to exist. I need a place where I can wear my beat up old torn red Keds sneakers, and not have anyone say, how can you wear those beat up old torn red Keds, get some new ones. I like my old Keds. They are predictable. I can count on them to feel the same every single time. So what if they get wet, they'll dry right back to the way they were, comfy and set in their ways, just like me. I like comfy Rena. I'm set in my ways. That's how it was when we met, that's how it is now, and that's how it will always be. We will always have separate huts, and that's just the way it is my love."

We were together for three years—three glorious, beautiful, amazing and heartbreaking years. We loved, we laughed, we sang, and we danced—Carly's talent soared, and my creativity rose beyond my wildest dreams. In our love, we connected on an alternate plane. Together we transcended to a place of tenderness that left us breathless and wanting more. In our differences, we descended to desolation and wretchedness, in our inability to change for the sake of the other, for the sake of our relationship, and for the survival of us. Instead, we continually disappointed each other until it's looming overshadowed it all. When we parted ways, we were a mere shell of our former selves and lost in our capacity to coexist.

When the all-inclusive hotel chain called to say they wanted to hire me as their in-house DJ, I was shocked. I could write my ticket to any resort anywhere in the world. Like a gut feeling that revealed itself, I said the first thing that popped into my head, Bora Bora in the Tahitian Islands of French Polynesia. My one condition, my beloved cat Barton gets to come along.

My sweet Barton was already on his way with a one-day layover in Houston. We'd arrive at Papeete Airport within an hour of each other. I couldn't wait to see him and hold his warm furry body to my heart, while we both purred. This little guy was all I had. My only family, my only love, in many ways my only friend. I'd spent the last two years shutting down all the feeling parts of myself and shutting out anyone I'd ever loved. I got tired of hearing it was time to move on. I'd never move on from Carly, of that I was certain.

I arrived in Papeete feeling oddly optimistic. I hadn't felt this way in a long time and yet I could hardly pin this new found hope on anything tangible. Perhaps it was my fast approaching reunion with Barton. I found my way to the cargo area of the airport to collect my kitty. I answered all the required questions, presented all the necessary documents and thanked the desk agent as he handed me Barton in his tiny pet carrier. I carried my furry love into the restroom, closed and locked the stall, knelt down and opened the door to his cat carrier. As he poked his head out, I scooped him into my arms and snuggled him to my heart, breathing the smell of my kitty into my lungs. Finally, I was home. It had been over a month since I'd seen Barton. In as much as he loved his pet sitter, he loved me more. We are family.

"Soon Barton, we will be in our new home in Bora Bora."

I put Barton back in his cat carrier and found my way to the gate for my fifty-minute flight from Papeete to Bora Bora. Upon arrival, we were picked up and whisked away VIP style. I was pleasantly surprised.

When Barton and I arrived at the resort, the concierge led us to a comfortable seat in the open-air lobby where the Hotel Manager, Ms. Val Reilly soon greeted us with a smile, a cold juice drink for me and a dish of cool water for Barton. She handed me a grounds map, an employee handbook, a room key and said follow me.

As we walked through the property, the beauty of the resort and island astonished me. The grounds were alive with flowers, bright orange and green birds of paradise, delicate purple and white orchids, pink and yellow hibiscus the size of small Frisbees and lush grounds robust with palm trees and dense foliage in every imaginable shade of green. Clusters of over-the-water bungalows in neat and tidy rows, accessible by raised wooden walkways over the turquoise blue of the lagoon waters below, were scattered throughout the resort. In the background was the larger-than-life view and sharp peaks of Bora Bora's Mount Otemanu. I was wondering where the staff's dorm housing was when Ms. Reilly, I mean Val as she instructed me to call her, interrupted my thoughts to say your over-the-water bungalow is the one on the end of this walkway. It's Hut number eight.

I looked down at Barton through the vent in the top of his pet carrier swinging from my left hand, and thought, *Barton can you believe what you see, this place is gorgeous and an over-the-water accommodation for the hired help?*

I must have looked stunned as I turned to look at her and said, "Ms. Reilly…Uh…Val, you can't mean to say that my staff accommodation is one of these over-the-water bungalows?"

She said, "Rena, we call the staff accommodations, Huts not Bungalows. It differentiates the accommodation type for our computer systems. In reality, they are virtually the same lodging. Our property is an all over-the-water accommodation resort."

Up to this point, I fully expected our staff accommodations to include a row of dorm style shared housing on the windy side of the resort devoid of views and guests. We were after all the hired help. We continued to walk down the raised wooden boardwalk towards my Hut. I looked down and watched my feet move. I marveled at the turquoise blue water coming and going through the evenly spaced openings between the wooden boards of the walkway. It was like flashes of sparkling blue and green jewels in the glistening sun. We continued down the walkway to the end and entered Hut number eight.

We walked into a large bedroom-living room combo. The entire front wall of the Hut was glass doors with an expansive view of the shimmering lagoon, Mount Otemanu and a private over-the-water deck with a small set of stairs leading directly into the turquoise blue and light green colored water. The color variations were incredible, like nothing I'd ever seen before. The white sandy bottom was visible in the bright sunlight of the day. The bed was up against the left wall facing out into the room. The thick and fluffy white comforter had orange, purple, and yellow tropical flowers arranged across the bed in a heart-shaped design. In the middle of the room, there was a large glass coffee table and a sofa. As we returned to the interior of the hut from the private deck, we approached the coffee table. I looked through the glass table top noticing a section of wooden floorboards under the table had been removed and replaced with a large glass window, allowing full view of the water and sea life below the Hut. From the nearby sofa, you could sit in the comfort of your room while watching the tropical fish play, the color variations in the water, and the white sandy bottom of the lagoon through your private window on the floor of your Hut.

I put Barton down and let him out of his carrier to sniff around his new home. I excused myself for a moment following Barton until he jumped up on the couch and settled himself for a snooze. I barely heard Val as she explained the various amenities of the room. I was more and more entranced with the looming view of Mount Otemanu, an ancient volcano that rises to a twenty-three hundred foot peak from the surface of the turquoise blue-green lagoon into the clouds above.

I felt oddly at peace here and unusually calm. Since losing my love, my darling Carly over two years ago, nothing had ever felt right again. But now, standing here in this mystical place, I was suddenly relaxed. I looked at Mount Otemanu. It's looming peak surrounded by bright sunshine and blue sky on one side, and dark, ominous rain clouds on the other. This island, in many ways, was a contradiction of itself and yet it's opposing weather patterns had found a way to cohabit separately and together, all at the very same time. If only Carly and I could have found this middle ground? Val excused herself saying, "Dinner is at six. We'll finish your orientation after dessert."

I stood in the middle of the room with the doors wide open staring out over the deck to the shadows of Mount Otemanu. I felt unexpected emotion rise in my throat. I began to cry as a loud rumbling of thunder exploded in the distance. I heard a tapping and thought it must be a nearby worker repairing some of the loose boards we'd walked over. I took a deep breath of fresh air. While closing my eyes, I reached for the sky, as if I could hold the fluffy white and ominous dark clouds in the palms of my hands and meld them into one. I heard the tapping again. As I walked back into the main room of my Hut, the tapping got louder. Barton picked up his head and looked at me. I imagined him saying, "*Well Mom are you going to answer the door or what?*" I shook my head in a futile attempt to clear my head of my jumbled thoughts and feelings. It was then that I realized someone had been knocking on my door. *Who would be knocking on my door in the middle of nowhere on Bora Bora?*

As I walked to the door, I felt strangely nervous. The thunder rumbled in the distance as I reached for the doorknob, turning it slowly as I opened the door to my Hut number eight.

When the door opened, I was looking down at the feet of my unexpected guest. I saw a pair of beat up old torn red Keds. As my heart began to race, I notice at a closer look the right foot was a brand new shiny clean red Keds sneaker and the left foot was a beat up old torn red Keds. I felt confused and flustered.

As I lifted my head to greet the face of my unexpected guest, I squeezed my eyes shut in a futile attempt to undo fate. I began to realize what was happening and immediately dispelled it as a wishful fantasy. I closed my eyes tighter as my heart raced.

How could this be? How did she find me? Why did she find me? She left me in the shadow of our irreconcilable differences in an abandonment that nearly killed me. I can't open my eyes—I can't—I can't go through losing her again.

I began to shake, first slightly and then violently. I kept my eyes tightly shut.

It was then that I heard her voice and felt her touch. She fell into me steadying herself with the palms of her hands as they hit my chest and her fingers splayed across my breasts.

"Rena my love, I've missed you so," she said.

I stepped back a bit and gently slipped my thumbs under her palms while lifting her hands from my breasts and opening my eyes. There she was—my heart—my darling, the love of my life—my person. My Carly. I began to cry.

"But how? But why?" I sobbed.

Carly gently placed her index finger over my lips to silence me and then touched my cheek with the palm of her hand.

"What are you doing here Carly?"

"The question isn't what am I doing here? It's why are you here?"

She looked at me with the wonder of love that was still alive in her eyes as she said, "I am the resident Zumba Instructor and Entertainment Manager. I've been here for two years. When Val told me the resort was looking for a DJ, I—well—I—wanted you, needed you, had to see you. I thought well maybe this is a sign—that fate wanted us back together? And so I recommended you and hoped you would pick the Bora Bora resort as your new home. I asked Val not to mention I'd recommended you. She agreed. You were hired, and here we are."

"I never stopped loving you, Rena. I never moved on. I can never love anyone but you. You're my love. You're my heart—you're my person."

"Carly, I don't know what to say. I...I...I've never stopped loving you. From that day in the Burbank Airport, it's been you only."

"Oh Rena, I don't know how this is going to work, how I am going to be different for you and us, but I can't live without you?"

I fell into Carly's arms, closing the gap on our two-year estrangement. I placed my hands on her chest and immediately began to panic, trying to pull away from her as she tried to hold me close.

I can't lose her again. I will never survive it. I can't do this. I can't do this again.

As these thoughts begin to run rampant through my mind, I saw the Keds sneakers on her feet. One new sneaker and one old sneaker—and then I remembered her words on the day we broke up, the last time I saw her, over two years ago.

She said, "*I need a place where I can wear my beat up old torn red Ked sneakers and not have anyone say, how can you wear those beat up old torn red Keds, get some new ones. Well, I like my old ones because they are predictable. I can count on them to feel the same every single time and so what if they get wet, they'll dry right back to the way they were, comfy and set in their ways, just like me. I like comfy Rena. I'm set in my ways. That's how it was when we met, that's how it is now, and that's how it will always be. We will always have separate huts, and that's just the way it is my love.*"

I pushed these thoughts out of my head. She was trying—*she was telling me she was trying to be what I needed her to be—an old sneaker for her and a new sneaker for me.*

As if she sensed what I was thinking, she pulled me close. I relaxed as my arms hung at my sides then around her waist as she whispered in my ear and drew me to her, "Rena my love, we may not always have separate huts, but for now, I live next door in Hut number seven."

Sallyanne Monti is an author and editor. Her fiction and non-fiction short stories, articles, poems, and edited pieces have appeared in numerous anthologies, magazines, and newspapers. She is at work on her first full-length novel, a non-fiction memoir love story entitled "Light At The End of The Tunnel," to be released in 2018. In her spare time, she plays guitar and composes music. She lives in Palm Springs, California and Sedona, AZ with her wife, Mickey, and their doggies Sola and Zorra. Website: www.sallyannemonti.com

Now that you've enjoyed Volume Three in a Heart Well Traveled Anthology Series, be sure to pick up your copy of Volumes One and Two.

A Heart Well Traveled
Volume One
Tales of Long Distance Love Affairs and Unlikely Outcomes

Discover the many facets of romantic relationships as authors in Volume One of *A Heart Well Traveled*, unravel the trials and tribulations of long distance love affairs.

Each author, with their own unique style of storytelling, will leave the reader begging for more. Go from wild rides to gentle love stories, exploring the twists and turns lovers go through as they work to be together despite the distance between them.

Explore bonds beyond friendship, chance meetings, family drama, gender complexity, longstanding love and unexpected passion as lovers seek their happily ever after.

A Heart Well Traveled is a collection of short stories where women who love woman share the joys and challenges of long distance relationships.

Can love really conquer all?

A Heart Well Traveled
Volume Two
Tales of Erotica, Fantasy and Sci-Fi Love Affairs and

Unlikely Outcomes

Each unique short story in this supernatural anthology will transport you to a magical interpretation of romance as authors bring to life uncommon love affairs and out of the ordinary long distance relationships. Escape into the realms of eroticism, fan fiction fables, intergalactic intimacies, lunar love, mythical fantasy, and past lives revisited.

Is it fate, is it destiny, or is it one of those defining moments where the universe comes to a screeching halt as an epic love appears?

Other Anthologies by Sapphire Books Publishing

The One: Stories of Falling in Love Forever - ISBN - 978-1-943353-32-3

If lucky enough, we fall in love once in a lifetime.

Children's books and romance novels promise us an encounter with a beautiful, mythical love – a passionate lover that sweeps us off kilter and changes everyday life into happily ever after. In reality, most fall in love a couple of times throughout a lifetime. Yet, those relationships fail to fulfill the "forever" expectancy – they end. Still, we hope that love, true and eternal will embrace us. We hope that stardust will cover the banal when life becomes monotonous or loneliness grasps us too firmly when days fades to night.

Reading about love triumphant sparks desire for more than uninspired routine existence.

In *The One*, an assortment of writers chronicle the discovery of the one woman to share the rest of life's journey.

Everyone deserves happily ever after!

A Sapphire Collection - Our Stories Continue Vol. 1 - ISBN - 978-1-943353-49-1

We craft lives from memories, shared moments with others, and from our experience as beings in the world. Our stories emerge from fashioning bits and pieces of life together with imagination and putting these ideas into words. As writers, we build worlds, give birth to characters, and hope to create a portal into a new realm, a place of communion of ideas, where fiction is alive in the mind of the reader. That's the joy of having others read our work. Our stories continue in the mind of the reader. Stories become shared spaces of strength, joy, personal insight, and where the individual loses herself for a while in an alternative realm of her own creation.

www.ingramcontent.com/pod-product-compliance
Lightning Source LLC
Chambersburg PA
CBHW032007180726
48283CB00008B/2581